Four-time RITA® Award nominee **Joanne Rock** has penned over seventy stories for Mills & Boon. An optimist by nature and a perpetual seeker of silver linings, Joanne finds romance fits her life outlook perfectly—love is worth fighting for. A former Golden Heart® Award recipient, she has won numerous awards for her stories. Learn more about Joanne's imaginative muse by visiting her website, joannerock.com, or following @joannerock6 on Twitter.

The Forbidden Brother

JOANNE ROCK

MILLS & BOON

First published in Great Britain 2018
by Mills & Boon, an imprint of HarperCollins*Publishers*
1 London Bridge Street, London, SE1 9GF

Large Print edition 2018

© 2018 Joanne Rock

ISBN: 978-0-263-07871-8

MIX
Paper from
responsible sources
FSC™ C007454

This book is produced from independently certified
FSC™ paper to ensure responsible forest management.
For more information visit www.harpercollins.co.uk/green.

Printed and bound in Great Britain
by CPI Group (UK) Ltd, Croydon, CR0 4YY

To Lisa Rivard for the friendship, the party-bus rides and all the fun texts that make me smile. So glad we met!

One

Jillian Ross ordered a bottle of the house's best wine and tipped back in her chair at her table near the window. Considering that the bar, centrally located in downtown Cheyenne, Wyoming, was called the Thirsty Cow, and the best vintage available was a cabernet she could have picked up at her local grocery store, she was pleasantly surprised by how good the first sip tasted.

Maybe that was because Ordering the Best Wine Off the Menu was a line item on her list of One Hundred Life Adventures—a set of goals she'd composed during radiation treatments for breast cancer two years ago. She was determined to accomplish every single objective, and then some, now that she had a second chance at living. It felt incredibly satisfying to cross off another ambition, even if she wasn't in a five-star establishment. Just being in Cheyenne fulfilled another goal, since Seeing the Western States had also made the list.

Actually, the travel category accounted for almost a third of her line items, now that she thought about it. She'd hoped her new job as a film location scout would put her in the perfect position to see the world—or at least the United States. Too bad she was already at risk of losing this gig.

"Can I get you anything else, miss?" asked a tall, harried waiter in a T-shirt printed with the name of a local college. Balancing a trayful of beers, he set her bottle on the table.

Country music blared through the Thirsty Cow, the Friday night crush a mix of local ranchers and tourists, peppered with military personnel from the air force base. Jillian had driven in from Pasadena three days before to meet with a wealthy ranch owner—the reclusive and powerful Cody McNeill—to try to change his mind about allowing a film crew on his land. Her mission was hampered by the man's complete lack of presence online. How could she make a personal pitch if she couldn't get a direct line to him?

The formal written request she'd sent to his business manager had generated a tersely worded refusal. But Jillian's boss had fallen in love with the photos she'd taken of the Black Creek Ranch—photos she'd snapped before she'd known the land was so carefully guarded. She hadn't seen any posted signs. But now that she needed formal permissions to move ahead, the higher-ups in her organization wouldn't consider any of Jillian's plan B spots, pushing her to sign the deal and book the Black Creek Ranch. Now, she was in town to convince ranching magnate Cody McNeill to change his mind.

"I'm all set, thank you." Jillian lifted her glass to toast her retreating waiter. "This is perfect."

She would never drink the whole bottle on her

own, especially since she'd carefully avoided alcohol following her initial diagnosis. But she was at the two-year mark, damn it, and she liked the idea of having it on the table to top off the glass. Besides, who was she to question the wisdom of her One Hundred Life Adventures list, since it had been dreamed up under extreme duress?

She turned her attention to the notes on her tablet, studying who owned the lands abutting the Black Creek Ranch. Cody McNeill's father, Donovan, had divvied up some parcels for his three daughters and three sons, giving the McNeill family expansive holdings in all directions. Those adjacent properties had some similar features to the Black Creek, but none possessed the iconic old barn that Jillian's boss had fallen in love with. Still, there had to be something Jillian could do. Carson McNeill, one of Cody's brothers, owned a ranch next door. She typed his name into her tablet. And…bingo.

Carson, in direct contrast to his phantom sibling, had current social media profiles like the rest of the world. His posts were mostly updates about the ranching industry, but every now and then there was a photo of the man himself. These seemed to be posted mostly by other people, female people, but in light of the man's rugged good looks that was no surprise.

In a word? *Yum.*

In Jillian's brief time working in the film industry this past year, she'd run across all manner of handsome men. Carson McNeill was every bit as attractive as any A-list star she'd spotted, but his dusty boots, perpetual five o'clock shadow and generally mussed appearance lacked Hollywood polish. Which was a plus in her book. His dark hair, strikingly blue eyes and charming grin drew attention, no question.

One photo showed him lugging a keg off the back of a pickup truck in the middle of a golden hay field, a hay baler behind him, a handful of workers surrounding him. Another image pictured Carson at a local bar, long legs sprawled out, booted feet crossed, while he slouched in his chair and grinned at the women, plural, seated beside him. There was a photo posted by the local newspaper—a throwback shot—that showed a younger Carson riding a bucking bull in a competition ring, a crowd of cheering cowboys in the background. Jillian could swear the man was grinning even then, his body arced backward, poised to slam hard on the ground.

Surely this seemingly good-natured rancher could be persuaded to help her win over his brother? Pleased with the new discovery, she took another sip of her wine and leaned back in her seat again, allowing herself a moment to daydream while the music switched to a slow country ballad. As two-stepping couples took the floor and a blue neon moon dropped from the ceiling, Jillian thought through the possibilities. If she could secure Cody McNeill's permission to film on his ranch, she would ensure future work from her boss. And since this film location manager was well-connected in the industry, she might pass along Jillian's name to her friends as someone who could find key locations and had the cinematography sensibilities to know what a director was looking for.

That meant more work. New travel. Additional items crossed off her list. Even better, that meant more ways Jillian was kicking cancer's ass. And that was what she wanted more than anything. Triumph over the thing that had scared her—almost—to death.

She stared out the window overlooking the street, preferring not to dwell on romance and two-stepping couples while remembering a period in her life that had been frighteningly loveless. Her boyfriend at the time had bailed right after her surgery to remove a tumor. He couldn't deal with chemo, he'd said. Let alone the radiation.

That still got to her. *He* couldn't deal with it. Like he was the one having to slog through that hell and not her.

Closing her eyes to banish the old demons, Jillian took a bracing breath. When she opened them again, she had to look twice.

Because she could have sworn that out there on the street, in the rainy Cheyenne night, she saw Carson McNeill. Instantly alert, she craned her neck to follow his progress up the sidewalk. Decidedly handsome from the rear, the guy looked to be the correct height and build. His worn-in jeans were a feast for the feminine eye. His boots and his Stetson were the wrong colors from what she'd seen online, but a man could own more than one hat, couldn't he?

Jillian gathered up her tablet and maps and shoved them into her homemade cloth satchel. Finding a couple bills in her wallet, she tossed them on the table beside her barely touched wine. The server was getting one heck of a tip, since she couldn't wait around for change.

After darting and weaving through the crowd toward the exit, she levered open the door and stepped out into the rain. Just in time to see the fawn-colored Stetson disappear into a building a block up the street. She hugged her bag to her chest, wishing she'd taken the time to slip into her sweater. Cheyenne was windy on a good day, and during a rainy night, the gusts took on a brutal chill. Especially for a woman who still chilled easily. Sometimes she thought the chemo drugs would never fully leave her body.

She reached the building where Carson Mc-Neill had disappeared and saw it was another bar. Wrangler's wasn't nearly as busy as the Thirsty Cow, so when she stumbled inside, in a rush to escape the weather, the patrons seemed to notice.

All five of them.

Hank Williams was playing on the jukebox and the dude behind the bar, with a grizzled beard halfway down his chest, was no college student. The wiry old guy gave Jillian a nod and went back to pouring a beer for the only other woman in the place—a middle-aged lady dressed like a biker in a leather vest over her long-sleeved T-shirt.

Wrangler's definitely wasn't the sort of joint where Jillian envisioned smiley, social Carson McNeill hanging out. But there could be no mistaking a man that good-looking. He was seated in a corner booth, and he'd just laid his phone on the table, flicking on the screen with his thumb before scrolling.

Jillian didn't realize she was staring until the bartender called over to her, "Have a seat anywhere you like." He gestured with a sweep of his arm to the empty tables.

Feeling silly for having been caught gawking, Jillian scooted into a booth across from her quarry. He hadn't glanced up at her since she'd first walked in and she wondered now how it would feel to have those intensely blue eyes on her. Which was peculiar, given that she'd lost all her mojo where men were concerned.

Part of that was her former boyfriend's fault, since he gave men a bad name. But the majority of the blame belonged to her disease and the treatment that had left her feeling like a dried-out husk of a woman. She'd read the brochures on what to expect after dealing with her chemo and radiation, so she knew that feeling was normal enough, and as side effects went, it wasn't the worst of them. After all, what did it matter if sex and men held no appeal when she was focused on her career and her recovery?

But right now, stealing glances at the tall, well-built cowboy two booths away, Jillian could almost forget she hadn't experienced deep physical arousal in two years. Because the man was intriguing. He wore a blue T-shirt under his gray-and-white work flannel, and she found herself fascinated by the play of muscle beneath the cotton. The edge of his jaw, shadowed with bristle, made her wonder about the texture and feel of him.

Then, to cap off a night full of surprises, Carson McNeill glanced up from his phone and stared back at her. His blue eyes narrowed. A fierce, intensely male energy vibrated all around him. She felt the electric jolt from that single look on her skin, tingling its way over her arms beneath the featherweight sleeves of her blouse. Her breath hitched in her throat with a soft, startled gasp. She couldn't seem to pull her eyes away.

A shiver traced its way down to the base of her spine. But this wasn't the kind of shiver that came with a chill. This one brought an undeniable flare of heat.

Her throat suddenly parched, she couldn't speak. Only this time, it wasn't because she felt like a dried-out husk of a woman. As she stared at a man who could hold the key to her professional future in his hands, she realized that her long slumbering libido had finally made a comeback.

For a moment, Cody McNeill wondered whether the lovely redhead seated in the booth across the way had mistaken him for his twin.

His whole life, he'd witnessed women stare at Carson in just that manner—like he was the answer to all their fantasies. It was strange, really, since he and Carson were supposedly identical. To people who knew them, they couldn't be more different. Even strangers could usually tell at a glance that Carson was the charmer and Cody was...not. It was in the way they carried themselves. The propensity to laugh. Carson's easygoing, leave-it-to-tomorrow approach was a far cry from Cody's belief that the buck stopped at his desk.

But somehow the redhead hadn't quite figured it out yet. She had been watching him since she stepped through the door of Wrangler's. The local dive suited him, since the food was good, the beer didn't require a dedicated menu and he'd bought the building a month ago to remodel for a more centrally located ranch office. Tonight, Cody needed a retreat from his family—mostly his twin. They'd been at odds for weeks over the sudden appearance of their paternal grandfather, a rich-as-Croesus hotel magnate from New York who'd disinherited their father over twenty years ago. Carson wanted to make peace with the guy, while Cody had no use for someone who'd betrayed their dad. The arrival of Malcolm McNeill in Cheyenne was tearing their already fractured family apart, and Carson had to make things worse by inviting the old man to dinner at the main house on Creek Spill Ranch. Technically, the property belonged to their father, Donovan, even though Carson oversaw the daily operations.

That latest bit of disloyalty made Cody mad as hell. His twin was too busy having fun all the time to ever think about the consequences of his actions. Which, of course, was why Carson attracted the kind of wide-eyed attention the woman in the opposite booth was currently exhibiting. Carson said yes to every entertaining opportunity that came his way, whether or not it was the right thing to do. Normally, that ticked off Cody. But at this moment, with the vivid hazel eyes of an attractive female following Cody's every move, he had to ask himself why he played it straight all the time instead of taking a page from his twin's book. If Carson was here, he'd have the decidedly sexy stranger under his arm in no time.

Between the dark mood hovering over Cody and the realization that he wouldn't mind stealing away one of his brother's admirers, he did something he hadn't done since he was a schoolkid.

He pretended to be his twin.

"Would you like some tips on what's edible around here?" He tested out the words with a smile. The expression was as fake as the pickup line, but he'd seen similar patter work for his brother a hundred times.

Hell, he ended up sounding just like him.

The grin gave the words the right amount of easy irreverence.

But the petite beauty in the booth nearby appeared to be stunned silent. Although slight in stature, she had a powerful presence. From her warm, henna-colored hair to the vivid blues and greens of her butterfly-printed blouse, and turquoise cowboy boots that had never seen a day's work, the woman stood out. She shone like a light in the darkened bar.

"Edible?" The word was a dry croak from her lips, a belated response to his question. Her cheeks flushed pink with hectic color.

"On the menu," he clarified, withdrawing his own laminated copy of Wrangler's entree choices from the metal napkin holder. "There are some good options if you'd like input."

The way she blushed, he had to wonder what she'd thought he meant.

And damned if that intriguing notion didn't distract him from his dark mood. He couldn't remember the last time he'd made a woman blush, and the telltale heat in her cheeks sent an answering warmth through his limbs.

"I, um…" She bit her lip uncertainly before seeming to collect her thoughts. "I'm not hungry, but thank you. I actually followed you in here to speak to you."

Ah, hell. He wasn't ready to end the game that had taken a turn for the interesting. But it was one thing to ride the wave of the woman's mistaken assumption. It was another to lie, and Cody's ethics weren't going to allow him to sink that low.

The smile his brother normally wore slid from Cody's face. Disappointment cooled the heat in his veins.

"Are you sure you want to do that?" It was a shot in the dark, and he was surprised to hear the words fall out of his mouth.

"Do what?" She frowned, confused.

The music in the bar switched to an old George Jones tune, a surprise choice from the jukebox, which was as ancient as the rest of the place. But the slow tempo gave him an idea to put off a conversation he didn't care to have.

"Are you sure you want to talk?" Shoving himself to his feet, he extended a hand to her. "We could dance instead."

He stared down into those green-gold eyes, willing her to say yes. He needed three more minutes to let the remnants of this hellish day slide away. Wanted an excuse to touch this pretty stranger who blushed for no reason. She took so long deciding he thought she must be debating a good way to refuse him. But then, surprise of all surprises, the sweetest smile curved her lips, transforming her face from pretty to...

Wow.

It was like someone flipped a switch inside her, making her come more fully alive.

"That sounds great," she agreed with a breathless laugh. "Thank you."

Sliding her cool fingers into his palm, she rose and let him lead her to the dance floor. It was small and a little warped on one side, but then, they were the only couple out there. Cody turned her to face him before drawing her into the circle of his arms. She fitted there perfectly, even if she was a head shorter than him. It put her at the perfect height where he could have buried his face in her hair. The glossy red curls smelled like honeysuckle.

She tipped her head up to look at him as they began an easy two-step, moving together well enough. She let him lead, her feet mirroring his as he spun them in slow circles around the floor. The full sleeves of her blouse grazed his arms, gently clinging to him.

Sensual hunger stirred with new restlessness, reminding him of every single month he'd spent alone since his last relationship. All twelve of them, in fact. And he hadn't been remotely tempted by anyone after discovering his ex-girl-friend's faithlessness, a treachery she defended by saying he was "too cold" for a woman to love.

Tonight he was anything but cold.

"I like this idea," the redhead in his arms con-fided, her fingers flexing ever so slightly against his shoulder where she touched him. "I can't re-member the last time I danced with a stranger."

Stranger?

Cody assumed she'd mistaken him for Carson. Did she not know his twin, either? He wasn't sure how he felt about that. At first, he'd been just as glad to undermine his disloyal brother. But as his temper cooled, and the longer he held this vibrant woman in his arms, the more he appreciated the idea that Carson didn't have any kind of prior claim.

"You've improved my Friday night a whole lot, too." He liked the feel of her, his hand warming the cool skin through the thin blouse she wore. "It's been a long time since I've thought about anything outside of work."

Her eyebrows lifted. "Leading me to wonder what you could be thinking about right now." Her lips curved. "Admiring the Wrangler's decor? Or maybe remembering how much you like a good George Jones tune?"

He laughed appreciatively. "I do respect a bar that still plays a classic. But the vinyl upholstery in the booths isn't doing much for me in the decor department." His gaze skated over her features; he was looking forward to making her blush again. "And I was thinking about you more than anything else."

His directness might have caught her off guard. She nibbled her lower lip briefly before meeting his eyes. "I haven't been the center of anyone's attention in…a long time."

There was a story there. He heard it in her voice. Saw it in her eyes.

"You aren't involved with someone else?" He needed to be sure before he let this go on any longer. But his pulse was already thrumming. "I don't see a ring, but I have to ask."

"I am very much unattached." She shook her head, red curls catching the overhead light as she moved. "What about you? No one waiting at home?"

"The only ones who might be missing my presence right now are a couple of rowdy shepherds back at my ranch who would have preferred the night off." He swayed with her. Her knee brushed his now and again in a way that fired right through him. "But no girlfriend. No wife."

He respected that she asked, even though she

was clearly feeling the same spark as him. And now that those formalities had been cleared away, he could simply enjoy the moment. The completely unexpected pleasure of having a beautiful stranger in his arms. He didn't want to let go of her now. He wanted to take her outside into the fresh, rain-cleaned night and kiss her. See if she tasted as good as he imagined.

"The stars are aligning for us so far, aren't they?" She peered up at him with something like wonder in her eyes.

He couldn't remember a woman ever looking at him quite like that. As if he was the answer to a question. An answer that pleased her.

"It feels that way." He didn't want to scare her off with empty pickup lines, or come across as some lowlife playing games with a woman in a bar. But as the music shifted again—this time to an even slower, modern country love song—Cody wondered if he could convince her to let the spark between them run wild. To follow the heat wherever it led. "And since the stars aligning would be a first for me, I wonder if can ask you just one thing."

He halted them in the middle of the floor, now that the two-step was done. Bringing her fractionally closer, he swayed to the slower tempo in a barely moving lovers' dance.

She followed him seamlessly, her gaze never straying from his. She was fully focused on him. Framed by dusky brown lashes, those green-gold eyes reminded him of new grass and spring.

"Sure. Ask away." Her voice had a sweet-sultry quality that made him want to listen to her speak more.

"Don't you ever wish you could forget about the expectations of the world around you and just… choose your own adventure?" He remembered books like that when he'd been a kid, where you could test out different endings to a story.

For someone who'd always taken the safe route in real life, he had liked the option of seeing how another choice played out. At least in a book. Cody couldn't do that with ranching. Or his family. But he could take a chance here. Tonight.

Her lashes swept down for a long moment, hiding her expression. But when she tilted a glance up at him again, there was a new curiosity there.

"Are you asking to share an adventure with me?" She sounded disbelieving. But maybe a little intrigued.

"I suppose I am." He would never have made such an outrageous suggestion to a local—a woman who knew him or his family. But she had *tourist* and *temporary* written all over her. Surely there couldn't be any harm in drawing out the flirtation? "What would you say to throwing away the rule book for a little longer?"

He let go of her hand for a moment to tip her chin higher, to see her face in the dim overhead light of the dance floor. Feminine interest flickered in her eyes. He inhaled as she released a pent-up breath. He could almost taste her in the space of silence between them.

Then he leaned closer to press his cause. "Choose me tonight."

Two

It was kismet.

Normally, Jillian wasn't the kind of woman who jumped on the fairy-tale bandwagon. Cancer had shredded every last romantic notion she had about the world and her place in it. These days, she was a realist. A pragmatist.

But how else could she view this man's suggestion that she choose a new adventure with him, at a time in her life when she was desperately rewriting her personal script to embrace new challenges? She owed her sanity and maybe even her physical health to that list of life adventures she'd written.

So for Carson McNeill to somehow tap into the deepest hunger of her soul and suggest they throw out the rule book, Jillian knew there had to be some kind of cosmic destiny at work. Call it providence, or maybe luck. Surely she could table her business agenda—just for a little while—to pursue this off-the-charts attraction? Once he'd rolled out the idea of an *adventure*, her personal mantra this year, Jillian saw it as a gauntlet thrown down by the hand of fate.

She was powerless to refuse.

To say nothing of how deeply attracted she felt to the man. She hadn't experienced the shimmering warmth of desire coating her skin this way since...ever. There was no precedent for the wobbly feeling in her knees. The light-headedness and the tingle over her scalp. The rest of the barroom faded away.

Her business with the McNeills would have to wait.

And if this turned out to be a mistake, she'd

have to find another way to get to Cody McNeill that didn't involve this very charismatic brother.

Simply put, if she didn't say yes to this moment, she would regret it forever.

"Yes," she answered him. Smoothing her hands over his flannel shirt, Jillian let herself inch a fraction closer. "I'm game."

It would be an adventure, but a safe one. She had her own car parked outside. She would text a friend her whereabouts. Besides, she had the reassurance that Carson McNeill was a respected member of the ranching community. A well-known, well-liked local. She'd scanned his entire social media profile just moments ago.

His masculine smile of triumph made her toes curl, sending an answering heat smoking through her.

"I can't wait to kiss you," he whispered in her ear. The brush of his mouth so close to her neck was tantalizing.

"I like where this is going." She swayed to the music there in the corner of the bar, the scents of beer and wings distracting her from the occasional hint of his aftershave when she got close enough to him. She thought about tucking her head against his chest and breathing him in, but she was already pushing the envelope. "Even though this would be the first time I've ever kissed a total stranger."

"I'm going to be heartbroken if you're backing out of this adventure already." The deep tone of his voice vibrated in her chest, making her tremble.

Another couple joined them; the woman who'd been sitting at the bar earlier tugged a rough-looking cowboy onto the floor with her. Their weaving, unsteady dance made Jillian's partner tighten his grip protectively, his hand splayed low on her spine.

Her heart rate quickened, her breasts brushing against his chest, sending an ache through her.

"Not a chance. Besides, I already know some things about you," she reasoned, recognizing that she couldn't get much nearer to this man without appearing positively indecent. Their thighs grazed together now and again, the contact reminding her how long it had been since her legs had tangled with a man's.

Too. Damn. Long.

"Is that so?"

"You like dive bars." She wondered why he'd come here alone. All his photos online showed him surrounded by friends—men, women, employees, coworkers.

"And redheads." Gently, he tugged one of her newly grown spiral curls, a hint of a grin playing at the corner of his lips. "Actually, I never knew how much I liked this fiery color of hair until tonight."

His gaze seemed to follow his fingers as he toyed with the ringlet for another moment, and her heart faltered at the sweetness of the gesture. Or maybe it was simply the affirmation that he enjoyed the crazy curls she didn't dare tame with hair product, fearful she would somehow lose the fragile regrowth.

Her throat dried up again. This night and this man were was making her feel things. Arousal. Romance. A giant dose of normal. She blinked fast to banish the sudden rush of emotion, unwilling to ruin things with an attack of weepiness. She would enjoy every second, damn it. Except the wellspring of feelings was already bubbling.

Gratitude for her new lease on life.

Joy in the simple warmth of a man's caress.

And yes, the return of physical longing, a keen hunger for more.

Unsure what to do with all that, and worried she would do something mortifying—like burst into tears on the side of the dance floor—Jillian rose on her toes and channeled all the sentimental burn into a kiss.

She could tell she'd surprised him. For a split second, he went absolutely still. Was he thinking she was crazy? Sex-starved? She closed her eyes to shut out those fears and simply let herself concentrate on the feel of his mouth on hers. The bristle of his jaw against her skin. The contrasting softness of his lips, which were full and sensual. He smelled like cedar and pine, woodsy and earthy, as if he'd been outdoors all day.

Just when she would have pulled back, however, the kiss changed. He became fully engaged, taking over her tentative efforts, which had been more about hiding her emotions. He pulled her into him, anchoring her body with his while he let his hands and tongue roam.

An onslaught of sudden, acute physical awareness put a stop to all her distracting emotions. His new command of the kiss allowed her to follow his lead, just like when they'd danced. Her head tipped back, her knees gave way. She wound her arms around his neck to hold herself steady, and to feel the full impact of his hard, muscular body.

Lost in the moment, she arched into him. Hip to hip, breast to chest. She needed full contact and she needed it now. Maybe he could tell as much, because he broke away from her suddenly, staring down at her while expelling his breath in a rush. With his hands on her shoulders, he steadied them both, since he seemed as surprised by the moment as she was.

The music had changed. A more modern country rock tune blared from the speakers and they were alone on the dance floor again. A waitress sidled past with a trayful of food; the scents of tabasco and beer were heavy in the air.

All that was secondary to the desire coursing through Jillian's body like wildfire, the red-hot sensation that was totally foreign, since her libido had been on ice for over a year.

"You see that door over there?" he asked, tipping his forehead so close to hers they almost touched.

She followed his gaze to the exit marked Private.

"Mmm." She nodded, since her voice wasn't working. Her lips were more inclined to kiss than speak.

"My offices are just through there and up a staircase."

"You work in the bar?" She didn't think that could be true. Wasn't he a successful rancher with considerable acreage?

"I bought the building and rent the space to Wrangler's. I'm remodeling the upper floors for... my business." He hedged about his line of work.

But of course, she already knew what he did for a living.

"How convenient to work close to a bar you like," she observed, not sure what else to say. Her thoughts were muddled from the kiss.

She wanted another one.

"It is," he agreed. "But right now, I'm thinking about how much privacy we could have for another kiss, on the other side of that door."

"Oh." That was logic she could follow. "Yes. Just let me grab my purse."

He scanned the bar, his gaze halting on the table where she'd left her bag, while she reached into her pocket for her phone. She texted a quick message to a friend to let her know where she was, taking basic safety precautions.

But if there was another kiss on the table, Jillian was taking it. And if that meant entering the backroom of a dive bar in a building Carson McNeill owned, that didn't deter her in the slightest. Her whole body hummed from his touch. She felt vitally alive, and that was a gift that neither her recovery nor the group counseling sessions she'd attended afterward had given her.

"Are you sure?" He paused and frowned down at her before they reached her table.

Perhaps he'd seen her text.

"I'm positive." She craved the adrenaline high his touch inspired. Thirsted for the physical contact that ignited sensations all over her body. Even before her chemo days, she hadn't experienced the kind of tantalizing thrill that contact with him provided.

Darting toward the booth, she retrieved her satchel. "Okay." She tried to restrain herself from leaping into his arms. Plastering herself to him. "I'm ready."

She didn't want to worry about work or filming on Cody McNeill's ranch anymore tonight. She just wanted to follow this adventurous path Carson had proposed, and hope it led her back toward joy and health. Well-being and wholeness.

Taking her by the hand, he drew her with him across the bar, past the dance floor and through the exit marked Private. He flipped a switch and an overhead lamp threw the space into view. As he closed the door behind them, Jillian's gaze immediately went to the vast office, which was still under construction.

The exposed brick walls and bamboo floors had been cleaned and restored. A staircase with dark slats and a thick, Craftsman-style handrail led upward, the mirror on the landing reflecting the dull light of silver pendant lamps. The beautifully detailed hammered-tin ceiling tiles looked original.

But she didn't have a chance to compliment him on the remodeling project in progress. He stalked toward her, his intent gaze rising from her mouth to her eyes. Her pulse quickened as she remembered why they were here.

The music from the jukebox drifted in through the open door. The rest of the world was close, but not close enough to see what was happening in here. He paused near her, took off his Stetson and settled it on a wrought-iron hook beside the door. She could see his eyes better now that the brim wasn't casting a shadow. Jillian let her satchel fall to the floor with a soft thud. Her eyes remained on Carson. The stranger she knew.

Then his hand was cupping her face, tilting her chin. Her eyelids fell, the sensations coming so fast and fierce she needed to focus simply on what she was feeling.

His kiss chased off any reservations she might have had, providing instant clarity about what she wanted. Desire shot through her; it felt like going up too fast in an elevator. Her knees almost buckled, and her whole body was seized with dizzying sensations. She reached to steady herself against him and ended up molded to the hard expanse of his muscles, from her hips to her breasts.

Her instincts took over. Winding her arms around his neck, she sought a closer connection.

For a moment, he kissed her harder. Deeper. She sucked air into her lungs in hard pants when he finally angled back, breaking the kiss to study her.

"Are you okay with this?" he asked, his thumbs stroking lazy circles on her shoulders through the thin fabric of her blouse.

She wanted more than a kiss, she knew now. Much, much more.

"Better than okay." She laid her palm on his cheek. Willed him to understand what she needed. Connection. Affirmation. Him.

His jaw flexed; his breathing was as labored as hers. Then he backed her into the wall and she vaguely registered the rough brick against her spine for a moment before he hooked an arm under her hips and hefted her higher. The action slid her along the rigid length of—

Oh. My.

She ran her fingers through his thick dark hair, clearing a path to his ear so she could whisper, "Don't stop."

Her soft plea undid him.

Up until that moment, Cody had been doing his damnedest to keep the explosive attraction in check. He'd made sure she was on board with what was happening between them. Helped her to feel safe and in control at all times. There was a bar full of people—well, a few people—just on the other side of the door.

But now?

She was like an out-of-control blaze in his arms. The chemistry was blistering. And her quiet, insistent "Don't stop" torched the last shreds of his restraint.

Cupping her sweet curves in his hands, he brought the juncture of her thighs against his rock-hard erection, feeling the heat of her right through her long skirt. With the flip of his belt buckle, he could be inside her in no time.

"Please," she murmured against his neck, kissing her way down his throat as she tugged at his T-shirt. "I have a clean bill of health. No partners since my last checkup." She stopped kissing him long enough to glance up at him.

His short bark of laughter surprised him. Hell, *she* surprised him with the glimpses of an efficient woman beneath the passionate kisses.

"Me, too." He set her back on her feet. "And thank you for that. I have protection somewhere. A bathroom upstairs, I think." He'd stocked the basics, since he'd spent a few nights here over-seeing the construction work when it had run late into the night.

"I have one," she blurted, scrambling to retrieve the patchwork bag she'd dropped on the floor. "I bought it when I—well, in a fit of optimism." She combed through the papers and electronics in her satchel. A bright pink pair of earbuds and a lipstick tube spilled out. "Here."

She stood back up and stuffed a foil packet into his right hand, then launched herself into his arms. He wanted to move them upstairs where there was a sofa, but her fingers made quick work of his belt and the button fly, scrambling the last of his good intentions as she stroked him lightly.

"Hold on to me." The words were a brusque command as he lifted her against him, a thigh in each hand as he helped her to wrap his legs around him. With her secured that way, he stepped close enough to the door to lock it.

She took the forgotten condom from him while he backed her against the door, a smoother surface than the brick wall. With her pinned there, he used a hand to tug her skirt higher. Out of the way.

She was in the process of tearing open the packet when he touched her through the silk of her panties, finding her hot and ready for him. He withdrew the condom from her, rolling it into place. His pulse pounded in his temples, the need for her an undeniable urge. A fierce ache. He wanted to take more time, touch her until an orgasm simmered through her. But her restless hands roved over him, peeling away his shirt and undershirt, tracing down his spine, spearing through his hair. Her hips bucked, and the slide of her soft, feminine center against his rigid length threatened to take his knees right out from under him.

Being inside her was his only option.

Slipping her panties aside, he entered her, slowly. Her fingers flexed against his arms, her nails gently biting into his skin as she held herself still. Head thrown back, she parted her lips on a sigh of pleasure. Her cheeks flushed deep pink, her lashes fluttering as she started to move with him.

The feel of her all around him was the sexiest high he could remember. From her boots hooked around his waist to her blouse sliding off one shoulder, she was all in. Her honeysuckle scent called to him, and he licked her tender skin while he buried himself deep inside her. Over and over again.

He held back when he could tell she was close. Her cheeks went from pink to small spots of red, her breath hitched and her hips went still. He slipped a hand down to touch her intimately, caressing tender circles right…there.

She came apart in his arms with a cry of pleasure that brought his release surging right afterward. Heat blasted his shoulders as sweat popped along his spine. The sensation went on and on, pummeling him, wringing everything from him. She clung to him, shifting against him as the aftershocks rocked her.

"Carson." She breathed the word with a sigh, her eyes closed and her head thrown back.

His brother's name on his lover's lips brought everything inside Cody grinding to a halt. His heart rate slowed. His brain ceased working, too. Nothing made sense.

"What did you just say?" His mouth formed the words even as a chill rushed over his skin. He shifted his hold on her, barely able to think.

She peered up at him through eyelids at half-mast.

Whatever she saw in his expression must have given her pause, because she tipped her head sideways and worried her lower lip with her teeth.

"Carson," she repeated, loud and clear, even though she looked abashed. "I'm sorry. I knew who you were when I walked into the bar. I was looking for you."

"Not me, sweetheart." With an effort, he straightened his shoulders. "I'm Cody McNeill. You've got the wrong twin."

Three

"You're Cody?" The color drained from the woman's face, as if that was extraordinarily unpleasant news.

Not that he was surprised. Cody did just fine with women when he chose to, but Carson had always been the ladies' man. Clearly, Carson was the guy she'd been hoping for. So yeah…he wasn't surprised, but definitely a bit disappointed given the incredible encounter they'd just shared. After his last go-round with a faithless female, Cody wasn't in the market for a woman who had her eyes on another man.

"In the flesh." He disentangled himself with an effort, setting her on her feet.

Only to realize, as he tidied up, that the condom she'd given him was now in shreds. The realization—coming hard on the heels of her mistaking him from Carson—sent him stalking to the other side of the work space and slumping down in a chair.

"Oh, no." The woman held her head in her hands. And she didn't even know the worst of it yet.

"Maybe you'd better have a seat." He used his boot to shove a second chair out from under the long, makeshift conference table that was a holdover from the retail store that had occupied the building long ago. "And tell me your name, for starters."

He'd had unprotected sex with a total stranger.

And while, yes, he'd started out wanting an adventure, he hadn't expected things to go so far. Especially not with a woman who had mistaken him for his twin.

"I'm Jillian." She lifted her chin and picked

up her bag before joining him at the table. She dropped into the utilitarian chair he'd offered her, her red curls drooping as much as her shoulders. "Jillian Ross."

The name sounded vaguely familiar, but he couldn't place it.

"Well, Jillian Ross, we've got bigger problems on our hands than you mistaking me for my younger twin brother."

"A twin." She repeated the word, shaking her head like she'd never heard of such a thing.

Cody steeled himself against the surprise kick to his ego and shared his more pressing concern.

"Correct." He heard his clipped tone and couldn't help it. "But right now, I'd like to direct your attention to the fact that the condom broke."

Her head snapped up, green eyes flashing even in the dim light.

"Excuse me?"

"Equipment malfunction," he explained, trying to keep frustration out of his voice. "Maybe the condom was past the expiration date?"

"No." She shook her head and then straightened her spine, seeming to recover herself a little bit. "I'm sure that's not the case, but it doesn't matter, since I'm disease-free, like I told you." She pulled in a quick breath and tipped her chin up. "And as for the other concern, there's a high percent chance that I'm…" She closed her eyes for a moment, as if gathering strength. Or patience. When she opened them again, there was a glitter in her gaze. A hint of emotion he couldn't fathom. "I'm most likely infertile."

He hadn't expected that. He ran a hand through his hair, his brain buzzing with unanswered questions. Questions he wasn't sure he should ask.

Then again, they'd taken a big risk tonight. He needed to know.

"How high a percentage?" He leaned on the conference table, only just now realizing he wore no shirt. He'd been so distracted he forgot to retrieve the only clothing they'd discarded before having sex. He spotted his T-shirt in a heap on the floor. "And how can you be sure?"

"I'm not comfortable divulging all my un-happy health history." Her words were clipped, possibly angry. "But I'm sure."

"I'm sorry for that. But you have to admit there's a lot at stake here."

"No." She shook her head. "There probably isn't."

Her shoulders were ramrod straight. It was a defensive posture. He told himself not to pursue the subject now. Not to push when emotions were already running high.

But then some of the tension seemed to seep back out of her. A sigh slipped from her lips.

"I've had extensive chemo and radiation, okay?" She held herself differently when she said it, arms crossed protectively over her midsec-tion. "My doctors warned me before we started that it was unlikely I'd be able to carry my own children. And not that it's any of your business, but I went so far as to freeze my eggs." Her jaw flexed. "So don't worry about it."

A stab of empathy had him reaching across the

table. Touching her forearm. He hadn't meant to unearth something so personal—so huge.

"I'm sorry."

"It's fine." She swallowed with visible effort. "I'm fine now." Blinking fast, she shrugged and pulled away from his touch. "I'm alive."

The quiet fierceness in her voice told him that fight had been hard-won. He wanted to know more about her—what she'd battled, how long she'd been in remission—but he didn't want to pry on a night when they'd already gotten under one another's skin in surprising ways.

"Very much so," he agreed, humbled by the small glimpse of herself she'd given him. "I didn't mean to encroach on something so private."

A wry smile quirked her lips. "You have a right to know, given the circumstances."

"Thank you." He appreciated her honesty and hoped it would continue now that he had another sticky question to ask. "So tell me, Jillian Ross, what exactly did you want with my twin when you followed me in here tonight?"

* * *

For the sake of great sex, she'd set fire to her career.

How could she have missed the fact that Cody and Carson McNeill were twins when she'd been researching their ranches? Jillian couldn't believe her bad luck as she stared across the table at the incredibly handsome shirtless rancher. Who'd be very angry with her when she revealed what she'd been trying to accomplish. She shouldn't have been plotting to gain access to one brother through the other, and she surely should have come clean before she committed to the sensual adventure.

Then again, why had Cody refused her request to film on location without any explanation or opportunity to plead her case?

"I thought Carson might lead me to you," she told him honestly. If she was going to lose the opportunity to film on the McNeill ranch altogether—and lose her job in the process— she would go out fighting.

"You wanted to find *me*?" He lifted a dark eyebrow, his brooding, skeptical expression not intimidating her so much now that he was shirtless.

She still couldn't believe she'd had sex with him. He held her professional future in his hands.

"Yes." Lifting her satchel, she laid it on the table and drew out the county land map. "I've been trying to contact you about this piece of property."

She pointed to the location where she'd taken photographs a few weeks ago.

"Black Creek Ranch." He spun the map to face him, smoothing the edges where it curled. "What do you want with—" He glanced up at her, recognition dawning on his face. "You're the location scout."

The tone of his voice made it sound like her job was in the same category as a tax collector's. His eyes lingered on her.

"One and the same." She smiled tightly. "I sent a letter to your business manager—"

"More than one," he reminded her, shoving himself to his feet. He prowled along the perimeter of the room until he reached his discarded shirts, and punched his fists through the arm-holes. "You asked repeatedly. But I don't want any film crews on my property."

"So you said in your two-line refusal." She knew she should be nice. Professional. But she'd burned that bridge when she entered the door marked Private.

"You didn't leave me any opportunity to explain how quickly we could finish the shoot, or the options we have for sending as few people as possible onto your land—"

"Because I'm not interested in having anyone on my land. That's the whole point of private property, isn't it? It's private. I don't have to let strangers trample all over it."

"But we're hardly strangers now, are we?" She hadn't been able to resist saying it. Her body was still tingling from incredible feelings—feelings she probably wouldn't get to experience again with him. She also thought about her list and all the adventures she wouldn't be able to accomplish if she lost her job. Real fear for her future rattled her. "Sorry. I didn't mean to have this conversation with you tonight. I—"

"You hoped to sweet-talk my brother into convincing me on your behalf?" Cody McNeill had put all his clothes back on, and the forbidding expression on his face made it difficult to believe he'd teased the best orgasm of her life from her just moments ago.

She remained in her seat at the conference table, unwilling to get too close to him when her fingers still ached to touch him. "I looked up who owned the property neighboring yours, since you're an extremely difficult man to reach."

"My work keeps me busy."

"Since Carson McNeill was easy enough to find online—"

"No surprise there," he muttered, reaching for his Stetson and planting it on his head.

"—I thought fate must be smiling on me when he walked past the Thirsty Cow tonight." She could really use the rest of that wine she'd left behind. Her head throbbed with a mixture of embarrassment and frustration that Cody didn't seem willing to give an inch.

She drummed her fingers on the tabletop, a blond wood that looked out of place in this very Western-style remodeled space.

"Except it wasn't Carson." His smile was a poor facsimile of the one he'd given her earlier.

Because, she realized, that hadn't been his real smile.

An idea took hold. A dawning comprehension.

"You were pretending to be him, weren't you?" She realized that initial exchange—when she'd first arrived in Wrangler's—was the only time she'd seen a genuine smile from him.

Except it hadn't been genuine at all. He had been imitating his brother. She could tell she had guessed correctly when a fleeting defensive expression crossed his face.

Indignation rose in her as she got to her feet and grabbed the map and her bag. She wouldn't be a fool for any man again after the way her ex-boyfriend had walked out on her after surgery. She was smarter than that.

"You know, I can take some of the blame for not telling you who I was tonight." She charged toward the door, ready to put this night—this obstinate man—behind her. "But it seems like you also played a role in this…misunderstanding."

"Misunderstanding?" He stood between her and the door. He didn't seem to be blocking it on purpose, he just hadn't stepped aside yet. "Is that what you're calling it? You came into town looking for a way to circumvent me."

She gestured at his imposing form with a flourish. "Sort of like I am right now, since you're still standing in my way. Apparently you take pride in being immovable."

His jaw worked silently; maybe he was chewing over the idea.

"That's not true," he said finally. "But I don't want you to storm out of here until I know you have a safe way home. And I'd also like to know where I can reach you tomorrow."

"Seriously?" She shook her head. "I'm perfectly capable of finding my own way back to the hotel. And I can't see why you'd need to reach me when you've made it clear you don't want a single soul on your *private* land."

He caught her off guard by reaching toward her and smoothing aside a curl that fell over her eyes. His touch, unexpectedly tender, reminded her of all the heat he'd roused in her before. What they'd shared had taken her breath away.

Even if he was being difficult and unreasonable now.

"First of all, I kept you out late and I want to at least walk you to your car, because that's what a gentleman does." His voice stirred memories of everything they'd shared, from a dance to so much more. "Second, I want to speak to you once the dust settles from tonight, because I owe you an explanation."

He had a point. She was dealing with too much sensory overload to wade through it all now.

"And third," he continued, opening the door that led back out to the bar, "we need to stay in touch because no matter what the doctors say about your fertility there could still be repercussions." He spoke in a low voice, his hand splayed across her back as they made their way across the dance floor toward the exit. "And I can assure you, if there are, I won't be a difficult man to reach."

Four

Cody knew he needed to head back home. He didn't usually grant himself perks like a midafternoon horse ride to clear his head—even on a mild, sunny Sunday like this one. But he didn't know how else to fix his state of mind.

His bad mood could be traced back to Friday night and the arrival of Jillian Ross in town. Then he'd spent an unproductive Saturday arguing with the company fixing the ranch's irrigation system. He'd handled it with so little diplomacy his contractor had walked off the job. Afterward, Cody had argued with Carson when his twin called to invite him to a Sunday noontime meal where Malcolm McNeill was going to be present.

As if he wanted anything to do with that branch of the family.

Giving Buxby, a retired stallion from the family's quarter horse breeding program, a nudge to the flank, Cody steered the animal through a thicket of cottonwood trees toward the stables at the Black Creek Ranch. He had done his damnedest to put the sexy and deceitful location scout out of his mind after he'd walked her to her car on Friday. But she'd shown up in his dreams both nights since then, and she'd barged into his waking thoughts, too.

He found himself remembering her laugh during a meeting with his ranch manager on Saturday morning. And recalling the way she'd murmured his twin's name at the peak of passion while Cody was directing the excavation for the irrigation system. He had been ornery and angry all weekend, and he blamed her.

He'd warned Carson about her presence in town when they'd spoken briefly on the phone this morning, skipping over the personal details of their encounter. Cody had thought it was important to let the family know that a Hollywood film company was angling to use McNeill land in a movie. He needed them to thwart her efforts, too. There was enough strife in the family over land rights and inheritance now that their estranged grandfather had entered the picture. Cody's dad hated Malcolm and wouldn't appreciate any of his sons or daughters breaking bread with their grandfather. But apparently, Cody was the lone holdout on that score. His half sisters had all decided Malcolm was a nice enough guy. Even Carson and their other brother, Brock, were coming around to recognize Malcolm McNeill as family.

That was fine for them.

But Cody's allegiance was to his dad, a man who'd built a ranching empire on his own, without any help from the billionaire who'd raised him. Cody not only respected that, he admired it. And if that meant missing out on a Sunday meal with his siblings, so be it.

As he cleared the cottonwood trees and came

within sight of the stables, Cody recognized the familiar silhouette of one of those siblings now. Scarlett, the youngest of his three half sisters, paced circles behind the stable, her red boots kicking up dust. Her long, dark hair spilled over the shoulders of a fluttery yellow blouse tucked into a denim skirt that was too damned short. She was talking nonstop on her cell phone.

When she noticed Cody, she quit pacing and ended the call, tucking her phone in her back pocket. Her dark bangs fell in her eyes as she peered up at him. She patted Buxby's haunch when he slowed the horse to a stop near the paddock.

"Is it true?" she blurted without preamble. "Is there a film scout in town who wants to do a movie at Black Creek?"

"Hello to you, too, sis." Hauling a leg over the stallion's back, Cody swung down to stand beside Scarlett.

He took an extra moment to plant a kiss on her forehead, stalling just because she was clearly beside herself and eager for details. The least he could do was wrest a small amount of fun from tormenting his sister. His other half sisters, Maisie and Madeline, wouldn't much care about a film crew in Cheyenne. But Scarlett had been born with stars in her eyes. While she could ride and rope as well as any woman he'd ever seen, she'd made it clear from the time she could talk that ranch life wasn't for her.

"Hello." Sighing, she arched up on her toes and landed a haphazard return kiss on his jaw. "Now, spill it. Carson said you met a location scout at Wrangler's on Friday night. Is she still in town? Did you find out what movie they want to make? Or when?"

Cody passed off Buxby's reins to one of the ranch hands' kids. Thirteen-year-old Nate was as excited about working with the animals as Scarlett was about moviemaking, and Cody had given the okay for him to help out in the barns as long as his dad was overseeing him.

"Make sure you brush him down thoroughly, and water him, too." Nate nodded as Cody kept talking. "Hang all the tack back where it belongs, and put the brush away afterward."

While the kid took over the care of the horse, Cody headed toward the main house. Scarlett kept pace beside him.

"Cody? I don't respond well to silence," she said as they passed her sporty silver Jag in the driveway. "And I drove all the way over here—"

"You live here," he reminded her.

They'd all been raised on the Black Creek Ranch. Carson had moved out long ago to run another of their father's holdings, the Creek Spill Ranch. And Madeline lived on site at the White Canyon, a small guest ranch. But all their places were within a dozen miles of each other.

Scarlett had remodeled an old bunkhouse after college when their father hired her to help the farm-operations side of the business. Technically, she was an assistant to the foreman. But lately she spent more of her time at the White Canyon with Madeline now that the guest ranch enterprise had expanded.

"But I hadn't been planning to come back here,

since I'm leading a fly-fishing outing for Maddy's guests later," she argued, following him into the equipment shed.

Halting beside an old International Harvester tractor he was restoring in his spare time, Cody turned on her. "That's some outfit for fly-fishing."

She grinned. "I'm glad to see your sense of humor is still in there somewhere." She poked him on the shoulder. "Now spill it. What's the deal with the movie?"

Leaning against the wheel of the tractor, she folded her arms and waited.

Cody entered the small space that served as an office and reached for a set of truck keys. There was a weather-beaten desk and a file cabinet they used to keep records on the vehicles. He took a seat on the desk. The shed was open to the elements on one side; the big overhead door was raised. They were alone, though, since most of the staff had Sundays off.

"I can't tell you anything about the film." He'd been far more interested in flirting with the stranger than asking her name, let alone asking about her job. Truth be told, he was mad at himself for thinking he could get away with some kind of anonymous encounter with a woman.

One-night stands were for other guys. He'd never been that person.

"Why not?" Scarlett asked, hitching the heel of her boot on the chair rung. "Didn't you meet the location scout in person?"

"I did." Which was an understatement. What he'd shared with Jillian Ross would be filed away in his memory banks for the rest of his days. "When she asked about filming, I told her absolutely not. End of story."

Scarlett pursed her lips. She had a big, expressive personality. Most of the time she was a sweetheart. Kind and thoughtful. Still, she definitely had a steely side that he'd rather not tangle with.

"You're not the only member of this family. I'm not sure that's your call to make." She straightened, putting both feet on the floor.

"Honey, I know you have stars in your eyes—"

"No." She cut him off with a fierceness he had

never heard from her. "Do not patronize me. Being feminine and having ambitions outside of this ranch doesn't mean I have stars in my eyes."

He drew a breath, wanting to apologize. To backtrack.

But she lit right into him again.

"Furthermore, did you ever consider how the exposure would help the White Canyon?" She planted her fists on her hips, warming up to her argument. "Madeline deserves that kind of spotlight, Cody. She's worked hard to make the guest ranch a success, and she's not the only one who would benefit from a film crew up here."

Cody cursed his twin for sharing the news with the rest of the family before he'd had the chance to. And yes, he cursed himself, too, for not making his stance clearer when he'd written to Jillian.

Although then he never would have met her. Never would have tasted her or touched her. And that he would have regretted. Even if he resented the hell out of her deceit.

"You're right. I'm sorry." He said the necessary words before his sister started in again. "I was only thinking about how Dad likes the privacy up here. You know how resistant he was to the guest ranch from the start."

Their father's fight against commercial development in the area had deep roots in his feud with his own father. When Donovan McNeill had first come to Wyoming and married Kara Calderon, they had soon run into financial trouble with her ranch, and had asked for his billionaire father's help, only to have Malcolm McNeill attempt to build a hotel on it. When Kara's father, Colt, protested, Donovan had nearly bankrupted himself hiring attorneys to untangle the mess and keep the peace. But the incident had created as many hard feelings between Donovan and his father-in-law as it had between Donovan and Malcolm.

When Kara died just a few years later, leaving behind three orphaned sons, Donovan had soon remarried, this time taking Scarlett's mother, Paige, as his bride.

And the land around the Creek Spill Ranch—land that extended all the way to the White Canyon—was still zoned to allow hospitality development, thanks to Malcolm McNeill's thwarted project. But to this day, Donovan didn't want anything to do with resort hotels. The guest ranch had come about only because he'd bought a failing bed-and-breakfast from a couple who were looking to retire and Madeline had wanted a shot at making it work.

"Dad doesn't make all the decisions for this family any more than you do," Scarlett reminded Cody. "We've diversified. Brock has the horse breeding business. Maddy has the guest ranch. Carson and you still work the cattle. But your business isn't more important than anyone else's in the family."

"Cattle brings in the bulk of the income." To an extent, each sibling's financial prospects were tied to the herd production, since all six of them owned a share. Their father had put some of his money in a trust for them, but the land and the businesses had been divvied up when the youngest—Scarlett—turned twenty-one.

"Yes, but since we each still have a stake in the Black Creek Ranch operations, we all have a voice in how it's run." Scarlett gave him an even stare.

"You've gone along with every decision I've made about purchasing bulls or negotiating prices on our calves, but now you're going to assert your authority over some film project you know nothing about?" Resentment stirred. He tightened his fist around the truck keys. He needed to move on with his day.

To put all thoughts of Jillian and her movie in the past.

"If I think the publicity could help us in the long run, you're damn right I'll assert my authority." She withdrew her phone from her pocket and passed it to him. "Now, would you like to write down the name and contact information for this location scout? Or did you want to give me the original letter she sent you and I'll track her down from that?"

If his sister were digging in her heels about anything else, he would have applauded her fierce defense of family and business. But Cody didn't appreciate her efforts when they flew in the face of what he wanted for the Black Creek Ranch.

"I don't know what I did with her letter." But he took the phone and typed Jillian's name on the notes screen. "This is her name, though. She was staying at the Cheyenne Suites last I heard."

He'd asked Jillian that when he walked her to her car, wanting to make sure she didn't have far to drive in the rain.

Scarlett raised an eyebrow, but didn't comment as she took back the phone and jammed it in her pocket.

"Thank you. I'll get out of your way now." Turning on her heel, she flounced toward the open door and out into the afternoon sun, the wind ruffling her dark hair.

He wanted to tell her that there was no way in hell he was letting a production company onto the family land, no matter what she said. Yet sometimes these disagreements fizzled out before he had to draw a line in the sand. With five siblings, he'd learned a few things about dealing with conflict over the years.

Still, seeing the determined set to his sister's chin as they'd argued told him it might not be that easy. He could only hope Jillian wanted to get out of town—and away from him—as much as he needed her gone. Their sizzling chemistry sure didn't pave the way for a smooth working relationship. Her deceit had only made it worse.

No matter how appealing he found the sexy film scout, she had played him from the start. And no amount of cajoling from his family or his baby sister would make that okay.

How dare Cody stomp on family opportunities without consulting a single one of his siblings?

Scarlett marched out of the equipment shed, phone in hand, to follow up on the film prospect her oldest brother had tried to ruin for them all. Did he have any idea how hard she and Madeline had worked to reach an audience beyond Wyoming? Or how hard Brock had worked, for that matter, to raise awareness about his quarter horses? The exposure a film could bring would make a huge difference to them all—and they'd be paid for it into the bargain.

Not to mention her own reasons for wanting this film to happen. She'd longed to get out of this town—out of ranching—for years. She'd tried to move to the West Coast after college to pursue an acting career, but her father had applied a first-class guilt trip, convincing her that she owed the family four years of her time and talent, since they'd financed her education. Too bad he hadn't made that clear *before* she went to Purdue University, since, with her grades, she could have gone to a state school for free—which would have eliminated his leverage for making her feel indebted to him. But okay. She'd ignored her urge to pursue acting and done the family thing like a dutiful daughter. Even though her relationship with her father had always been…tense.

She was the last of six kids and—in her father's eyes—one too many. He'd never made a secret of the fact that his daughters hadn't proved as useful on the ranch as his sons, although Maisie came close. Scarlett had stayed on here to ensure she worked off the cost of her education even though her family could easily finance half the state's tuition if they chose. She refused to be a trust fund baby.

But Scarlett's four years were almost up. And she was more than ready for something different. That acting career she'd once dreamed of wasn't out of the question. She could always go to Hollywood for a year and just see what happened.

Scarlett dialed the hotel her brother had mentioned. "I'd like to speak to a guest," she said when the clerk came on the line. "Jillian Ross, please."

Scarlett slipped through the back door of the old bunkhouse she called home. Her father had given her a generous budget to remodel it. At first she'd refused, knowing she didn't want to be stuck in Wyoming for long. But when he shot down her simple renovation plans, insisting he wanted the grounds of the ranch to have an updated look for visitors, Scarlett had thrown herself into the task.

Now the bunkhouse had higher ceilings with

exposed beams. The barn-style exterior had been modernized with heavy retractable doors that could be raised on temperate days. Tall posts supported the deep, extended roof that sheltered porches on two sides of the building. Indoors, an open floor plan allowed her to see the living area, kitchen and family room from the seat she took at the breakfast bar. She grabbed a sheet of notepaper from the sleek concrete counter as the hotel representative came back on the phone.

"Ms. Ross is not currently a guest with us, ma'am," the woman informed her. "We're not allowed to give out more information than that."

Damn it. Had she left town?

Thanking the woman, Scarlett disconnected the call and opened her browser to search Jillian Ross online. She found her profile immediately. A gorgeous redhead with short auburn curls... It was easy to find the name of her production firm.

Scanning the company's list of projects, Scarlett discovered a modern Western that might be the film Jillian was working on. For the heck of it, she did a search on that, too.

And found a man's name she knew well.

Logan King.

Everything inside her went still. It couldn't be a coincidence. She'd met him—then, a small-time actor—a few months ago on a flight to Los Angeles when she'd taken a shopping trip for her mother's birthday. They'd flirted. Kissed. Had an incredible surprise night together. She had thought it was about more than lust, and grew certain the feeling was mutual when they'd messaged each other for a few weeks afterward. Then he'd mysteriously stopped texting. Had vanished. She'd been ghosted.

Since then, he'd had a big breakout movie. She'd been slammed with images of him all over social media, endless reminders of how forgettable she'd been for him. How dispensable.

Could there be a chance he might really come here? To her home turf? Anger simmered through her all over again as she remembered their night together. The hurt of the aftermath. He'd made it clear that his Hollywood career was more important than a fling with her.

Her brain raced with half-formed revenge schemes, each more outrageous than the last. What she really wanted was to tell him off to his face. But in *his* hometown, not hers. She couldn't wait around for him to show up in Cheyenne, possibly with some new actress girlfriend on his arm. Somehow, she needed to tell him exactly what she thought of him before then.

She had to hurry and change for her fly-fishing expedition back at the White Canyon Ranch. But first, she looked up Logan on one of the star-watcher sites to find out where he'd been spotted last. Just in case one of her revenge schemes came together. She also left a message for Jillian Ross at her production company.

Because Scarlett's primary concern was making sure the whole family's interests were represented. There was no reason Madeline's guest ranch shouldn't benefit from the movie exposure. And maybe Scarlett would make some valuable contacts in the business, too.

But if she could also find a way to confront Logan King and tell him he could go to the devil? So much the better.

Five

Steering her rental car down a public access road that bordered Carson McNeill's Creek Spill Ranch, Jillian tried to picture the landscape standing in for the property where she truly wanted the film to be shot—Cody's Black Creek Ranch with that gorgeous, iconic barn as a backdrop.

It was tough to imagine her original plan coming together now. Not after what had happened between them. Cody had taken her number and told her he would call the next day, but all of Saturday had passed without a word. The silence shouldn't have bothered her, since she'd wanted a simple, no-strings encounter. And yet...she couldn't deny the sting that came with not hearing from him.

She'd checked out of her hotel room in town this morning, planning to register at the White Canyon Ranch tonight. It was yet another property owned by a McNeill sibling. The family possessed the second most acreage in the state, so they were a powerful voice in the ranching community. That could hurt Jillian's cause, of course, if they banded together and refused her request. But the McNeills were a large and disparate group of individuals with wide-ranging interests and pursuits. Surely one of them could be swayed to compromise with her. Two executives from Jillian's company had already booked flights this week to visit the location.

She couldn't give up her quest yet because this job was her means to an important end— her ticket to seeing all the places she'd promised herself she would go after her treatments. Life was too short to live in the shell she'd been stuck in before cancer struck.

Even though Cody had shut her down after their surprise encounter, she still had options. She could find a way to salvage this trip and keep her job.

Her cell phone chimed and she pulled off to one side of the road to take the call, high grass brushing the passenger door as the tires dipped onto the shoulder. She didn't recognize the number, but it was local.

"Jillian Ross," she answered, as she moved the gearshift to Park, wondering if her earlier inquiries had paid off. She'd left messages for both Carson and Madeline, hoping one of them could accommodate the film crew.

Or reason with their stubborn brother.

"Jillian." The male voice on the other end made her pulse quicken. "This is Cody."

He put the slightest emphasis on his name, giving the simple sentence a whole wealth of subtext. That subtle reminder about the identity mix-up, delivered in his sexy voice, stirred all kinds of feelings inside her. Resentment, maybe. A little embarrassment. And, no matter that she wished otherwise, a whole boatload of attraction.

"Hello." She rolled down her window before switching off the engine, wanting to feel the Wyoming breeze on her suddenly warm face.

"I hope I didn't catch you at a bad time."

"No." She stared out over fields of golden hay waving gently under the bluest sky she'd ever seen. There wasn't another car or person in sight. "I'm just surprised to hear from you after the way we parted."

She closed her eyes, breathing in the scent of roadside wildflowers. Yarrow and daisies. Some tiny yellow blossoms she didn't recognize. She was determined to take joy in this trip, even if she failed in her quest and lost her job. Her dreams of travel and adventure had gotten her through the darkest hours of her disease.

"That's why I'm calling." He paused a beat, and she opened her eyes, surprised. "To apologize about that. No doubt I overreacted."

Hope shot through her. Maybe he was giving her a second chance to film on the ranch? Or maybe he wanted to see her again? She really shouldn't want the latter. But she couldn't deny how the idea ran through her brain, tantalizing her.

"When you didn't phone yesterday, I assumed I wouldn't hear from you again." She picked at a loose thread on the leather steering wheel cover.

"Sometimes I'm slow to think my way through things," he admitted. "But my youngest sister made a point of reminding me I don't speak for the whole family when it comes to the McNeill lands."

So he was calling about the film. Part of her rejoiced that there was a chance he would reconsider. But she couldn't help a small twinge of regret that his call had nothing to do with what they had shared.

"Should I get in touch with your sister?" Jillian asked quickly, sweeping aside her disappointment that this wasn't a more personal conversation.

"Actually, I hoped I could give you a tour of the ranch," he offered, his voice a warm rumble in her ear. "Show you some of the drawbacks that might make you reconsider where you want to film."

She would see him again. A hidden, secret part of her feminine self stretched and preened like a satisfied cat. She closed her eyes to shut out the feeling, impatient with all the wrong-headed instincts that had landed her in his arms in the first place.

"But a tour might further convince me that the Black Creek Ranch is the ideal location." She wondered if she'd meet this sister he'd mentioned.

"I'll take the chance." He sounded sure of himself. "When would be a good time for you to come? How much longer will you be in town?"

"I'm close to the ranch right now," she admitted, knowing she could be at Cody's place in ten minutes, tops. "How's today?"

She was met with silence for a long moment.

"Today is fine," he said finally. "Drive straight to the main house. I'll meet you out front. Assuming, of course, you know the way here?"

He knew perfectly well she'd been trespassing when she had scouted the location the first time.

"I'll manage." She started the engine on the rental car, a surge of anticipation firing through her. "See you soon."

Disconnecting the call, Jillian contemplated her best approach. For starters, she'd take the scenic route to the Black Creek Ranch. No sense revealing she'd been lurking just around the corner from his property, contemplating how to get in touch with Carson.

Based on what had transpired between her and Cody Friday night, the news that she was still trying to meet with his twin wouldn't be well received.

She was excited to see him again, but she couldn't let that attraction draw her into doing something that would risk her job. And there was beginning to be hope on that front. Jillian might have allies in some of his siblings, particularly his sister. But she needed to work fast now that executives from her company were coming into Cheyenne this week.

She would be sharp, professional and keep an ear out for any way to get an agreement signed with the McNeills. And perhaps most important, keep squarely focused on business around the man who'd shown her a kind of physical pleasure she might never experience again.

Absently pulling a few weeds out of the cook's cottage garden by the main house, Cody steeled himself to see Jillian Ross again.

He'd had nearly two whole days to process what had happened between them and put it behind him. He hadn't.

If it hadn't been for Scarlett's objections, he wouldn't be seeing Jillian at all. He would have called, as he'd promised, but just to make sure their night together hadn't had consequences. He wasn't a careless man, and the way he'd lost his head with her that night didn't sit well.

Cody heard a car pulling into the driveway, followed by a sudden chorus of barking dogs. Straightening, he dusted off his hands and turned to see Jillian waving tentatively at the animals from the driver's side of her car as she parked.

Cody whistled, bringing the two border collies and the Australian shepherd to his side while Jillian got out of the vehicle and strode toward him. She was as colorful as he remembered. The red hair and bright turquoise boots were the same as the other night. But today she wore dark jeans and a tan blouse with Aztec designs embroidered in green, red and yellow beads around the tassel ties down the placket.

"Thanks for calling off the dogs." She grinned down at them. "They looked friendly, but I wasn't sure what they thought of strangers. May I pet them?"

The canine trio looked longingly at her, tails wagging. At least they minded their manners, sitting still for the moment.

"Sure. Start with Hammer." Cody pointed to the Australian shepherd. "He sets the tone for the younger two."

"As older siblings do." She met his gaze, her hazel eyes teasing. Then she turned her attention to the dog, scratching him behind one ear. "Hello, Hammer."

"How did you know I was the oldest?" He wondered how much research she'd done on the family in her quest to access his land.

"I didn't." She petted the collies as they hopped up to meet her without being asked. "I just knew you were the older twin because you mentioned it the other night."

He didn't recall that, but then, he'd been fairly preoccupied.

"That's Gomez and Morticia, by the way." He pointed out which dog was which and she patted them briefly before they trotted off to seek shade. "The younger ones never think the rules apply to them."

"Is that so?" She tucked a springy curl behind one ear as she faced him.

Something about the gesture triggered a vivid memory of Friday night, of his face buried in that honeysuckle-scented hair, her arms twined around his neck as he kissed her deeply. Blinking, he forced aside the thought.

"Are you a younger sibling?" He waved her toward the equipment shed, where he'd gassed up one of the Gator utility vehicles to show her around.

Hammer rose, too, following Cody, as was the dog's habit.

"I'm an only child, so sibling dynamics fascinate me." She walked quickly beside him, making him realize he was burning a path to the shed like he was being chased by a grizzly.

He slowed down, leading her to the small lot beside the shed where the two-seat vehicle was parked.

"Well, I've got two younger brothers, my twin and our other brother, Brock. Then I have three half sisters from my father's second marriage—Madeline, Maisie and Scarlett." He glanced over at Jillian as she stared at the Gator. "I thought I'd drive you around the ranch. Unless you'd rather go on horseback?"

It hadn't occurred to him she might ride.

"This is fine." She nodded. "I've just never seen anything like it. Sort of a modified lawn tractor?"

He laughed. "Hardly. Hop on." He proceeded to take his own seat behind the wheel. "We use this to get around the property quickly, especially for hard-to-reach places where a truck is too heavy. It's quick and economical."

"It looks like you have your own fleet in there." She pointed to the equipment shed, where he kept the tractors and trucks.

"Most days, those are all out in the fields and pastures, but it's quiet around here on Sundays." He switched on the Gator while she fastened her seat belt. "And that brings me to the first of many dangers of ranch life I'll be pointing out on the tour today. Accidents happen all the time with heavy machinery, especially when untrained people are around. Visitors get too close, the operator can't see them and the next thing you know, there's a serious injury."

He knew too many people who'd lost fingers, toes or whole limbs to accidents. She needed to understand why filming around here could be dangerous.

"Maybe we could get most of our shots on a

Sunday when it's quiet." She reached for the roll bar on the passenger side while Hammer jumped into the cargo bed behind them.

Cody stepped on the gas, holding back the argument that rose to his lips. His sister would get on his case if she found out he was being too difficult, so it wasn't wise to alienate Jillian before they even got under way. Besides, given the way they'd parted at Wrangler's the other night, he figured it made sense to smooth things over with her. He'd been speechless after what took place. And once he'd learned why she couldn't have children, he'd been so caught off guard he had forgotten to ask about taking the extra precaution of a morning-after pill. Hell, he hadn't known what to say, period.

For now, he focused on driving Jillian around the spread, pointing out some of the outlying buildings and pastures. She asked a few questions about the hay fields and the different breeds of cows, but mostly she seemed to take in the long views. Every now and then she would snap a few photos on her phone.

"It seems idyllic," she observed while they watched a herd of cows grazing on a green hill.

"It's nonstop work." He'd kept her away from most of the ranch activity today, not wanting to get in the way of the foreman and a few others who were putting in hours on the weekend. "And believe me, it's dangerous."

He couldn't give her the impression the ranch was just some scenic spot for touring around.

"You mentioned the equipment."

"Plus the weather. And the animals." He hadn't wanted to share his personal nightmare, but she still seemed convinced this place was nothing but the perfect backdrop for the movie she had in mind. "My mother grew up on a bigger spread than this. She was an experienced rancher. And that didn't save her when she tried to separate a bull from one of the cow pens."

He'd been only four years old at the time, but the memory of seeing his mother downed by that bull had been burned in his brain. He hit the gas harder, but knew he'd never outrun that memory.

"You mean..." Jillian turned her head to him. He sensed the movement even if he didn't see it.

"She died from her injuries three days later." Cody and his brothers had filed into her hospital room to say goodbye. He couldn't recall what he'd said to her. He only remembered his father sitting in the chair beside her—shell-shocked and white as a ghost as he stared at his dying wife.

"Cody, I'm so sorry." Jillian touched the back of his hand where it rested on the steering wheel. "How frightening that must have been for you and your brothers."

He ground his teeth, unwilling to accept condolences for something that should have never happened in the first place. For something preventable. "It taught me to respect the animals and the land."

He glanced at her, hoping she recognized the dangers better now. Her eyes were filled with empathy. But this wasn't about his loss. It was about safety.

Jillian's hand fell away and she nodded. "I understand."

"Good." He didn't want to dwell on the past. He just wanted her to find someplace else to shoot her movie. Somewhere that wouldn't pose risks to her film crew or to his own workers. Or his cattle, for that matter. He hoped he'd talked her out of her plans by telling her about his own tragedy.

They continued the tour. About ten minutes later, he stopped the vehicle, and she stood up and turned three hundred and sixty degrees, shielding her eyes from the sun as she drew deep breaths. He couldn't help but be drawn to her.

"What do you think?" he asked. They were near a shallow creek between grazing fields. He was resting this pasture now, giving the plants time to regenerate. There wasn't much to see.

She stood tall beside him, resting her elbows on the high roll bar as she looked out over the hills.

"I know it's a dangerous place, but I still think it's incredibly beautiful." The warm sincerity in her words stirred something in him. Sunlight turned the tips of her hair yellow, giving her a special glow. "I've never seen so much nature. So few people." She tipped her head sideways and glanced down at him. "I'm used to crowds everywhere, and this is just so peaceful."

He nodded, understanding. And he was grateful to have moved the conversation away from his past. "Whenever I go to Denver or Dallas—any of the bigger cities where we have business—I think about that. How there are too many people and not enough of this."

They shared a moment of common ground, soaking in the serenity of the ranch. This was why he was determined not to unleash a film crew on this quiet land. Not to trample the beauty.

Beside him, Jillian let go of the roll bar and lowered herself back into the seat. Hammer jumped down from the cargo bed to sniff around in the weeds.

"I took this job to travel. To see things like this." Her hazel eyes, more green than gold in the sunlight, remained fixed on the horizon. "I realized last year that travel is really important to me."

The sense of kinship with her faded as Cody realized she wasn't taken by *this* land so much as seeing new places. Jillian Ross wouldn't be sticking around Cheyenne, no matter how beautiful she might think it was.

"Because of your illness?" he asked, remembering what she'd said about the radiation and chemo. He'd been curious Friday night, but it hadn't been the right time to ask.

Was now the right time? He wasn't sure where any of this would lead with her, but if there was any chance she carried his child, he would need to get to know her much better. And even if she didn't, he at least wanted to stay in touch with her for the next few weeks—until she knew for sure one way or another. He couldn't afford to alienate her.

She nodded once. A quick affirmative. "I made a list of life adventures." He recognized the defensive stance as she folded her arms around herself. He'd seen it that night in his office when she'd admitted she couldn't have children. "It seemed like a productive thing to think about during my treatments. A way to focus on something positive."

He couldn't imagine what that must have been like for her. And she had no siblings. Had her parents been with her? A partner? If she'd had one then, he obviously hadn't stuck around long afterward. A surge of defensiveness on her behalf moved him to place a hand on her shoulder, offering whatever comfort he could for a memory that must be painful.

"I'm sorry you had to go through that." He wasn't sure how much to ask about it. "Have you been in remission long?"

A sad smile pulled at her lips while she watched Hammer take a half-hearted nip at a butterfly. She shook her head. "I won't be considered in remission for three more years, so I've got a long road ahead of me yet."

"Ah, hell." He squeezed her shoulder through the thin blouse. It didn't compute that this vibrant woman could be so vulnerable. "I didn't realize…"

"Of course not." Her smile, though still sad, was more genuine this time. Her hand landed on his knee. "You couldn't possibly know. It's awkward for people to talk about, but I appreciate you acknowledging my journey. Breast cancer—any cancer—is scary."

No wonder she hadn't been worried about pregnancy. Her body had been through hell, and not all that long ago. He regretted raising a topic that had to be difficult for her. For a moment, the only sound was a plane far overhead and the snuffle of the dog as he searched the grass.

"So you fought back by plotting your life's adventures." Cody's fingers stroked the nape of her neck, the skin barely covered by her red curls. New hair, he guessed. Regrowth after her treatments.

All of her seemed suddenly more fragile, even though he guessed she would hate that description. Her eyes mesmerized him. Her lips parted for a moment when he caressed the side of her throat, trailing a knuckle behind one ear. The touch that began as comfort had become something else entirely.

"It started out as me daydreaming about things I wanted to do. I'd gone to school for accounting and I'm good at it. But I did it because it was reliable—good job security and a decent living." Her fingers curled on his knee, squeezing lightly through the denim. "Once I got cancer, though, I asked myself if that was enough reason to do something I didn't really enjoy for one third of the hours in my day."

"And you decided it wasn't." A gust of wind slanted the grass in the pasture. Hammer sniffed the air before returning to nosing the ground.

"Not at first. It took weeks of me thinking about all the other things I wanted to do with my life if I had the chance to do it over again." She stared down at her hand where it rested on his knee. "Then, one day when I was sick out of my mind and miserable—my personal cancer rock bottom—I decided I owed myself that do-over. If it was in my power to make it happen, I would."

He couldn't possibly know how hard that battle had been for her. But he admired her strength and conviction.

She straightened in her seat, her hand sliding away from his knee, the moment of connection broken. Or maybe she simply didn't want to share any more with him. They'd had a sizzling encounter together, but they sure didn't know each other well.

Against his better judgment, however, Cody found himself wanting to know more about Jillian Ross. He couldn't seem to force himself to pull his fingers from her neck. His hand lingered the same way his thoughts did—on her.

"And here you are." He watched the way the sunlight played on her pale skin. "Living your adventure on a ranch in Cheyenne."

"It's a long way from Reseda, the Los Angeles neighborhood I grew up in." She pointed toward a pronghorn buck emerging from a thicket at the edge of a field. "I need a photo of that."

Digging in her leather handbag, she came up with her phone. Cody forced himself to slide his hand away from her while she lined up the image she wanted on the view screen. After she snapped a few pictures, she tucked the phone away and they watched the buck stalk across the field. Cody saw all kinds of deer and elk around the ranch frequently enough, but it had been a long time since he'd simply sat and watched something like that. Her breathless appreciation made him see the common sight with new eyes.

He whistled for Hammer, putting the utility vehicle in motion again after the dog hopped in back.

"Can I ask what other adventures are on that list of yours?" Cody asked as they headed back toward the main house. He hadn't gotten to all of his concerns about the dangers of ranch life during this tour, but now wasn't the right time.

His sister's concerns that he'd shut down the film crew without consulting anyone else had resonated. He wanted to at least be able to tell Scarlett that he'd taken the time to show Jillian around without scaring her off completely.

That didn't mean he'd changed his mind about hosting a movie production at the ranch. Still, even if she was sure that pregnancy wasn't a possibility for her, he planned to keep her close for the next few days. Just until he could convince her to get a blood test and rule out the chance of a baby.

Besides, he couldn't deny an interest in the film scout. Spending more time with her wasn't going to be a hardship.

"Mostly travel, but there are some other experiences I've never had that are on the list." She began counting things off on her fingers. "Hear a world-renowned symphony orchestra in concert. Take a ballet class. Study Italian. Bungee jump. See a rodeo—"

"A rodeo?"

"I've never been to one." She shrugged. "It sounds fun."

"You know Wyoming is the called the Cowboy State for a reason." He pushed the gas pedal harder as they got back onto well-traveled roads closer to the house. Hammer stuck his nose between them for a better view ahead.

"I've seen a wealth of Stetsons since I stepped off the plane." She reached over to stroke the dog's head.

"And they're converging on Cheyenne for

Frontier Days. The bull-riding finals are in town this week, the biggest rodeo of all."

"Really?" She peeked at him around Hammer's head. "I saw some signs about that, but guess I didn't look too carefully at when it took place."

"Maybe you should stick around town a little longer so you can cross another adventure off that list." He drew to a stop in front of the equipment shed not far from her car. The shepherd jumped down from the cargo bed, leaving the two of them alone.

Jillian's eyes veered to his, her windblown curls teasing her cheeks as she seemed to weigh the idea. "That sounds fun. And I was thinking about checking out your sister's guest ranch, anyhow."

So she'd been planning to stick around. Of course she had. She wasn't giving up so easily on her plan to talk him into hosting the film crew. Although she would go home disappointed on that score, maybe they could make a few other pleasurable memories. The attraction between them sure hadn't dimmed.

"Tuesday night, then." He skimmed a touch

over her cheek, just enough to brush away a curl.
He liked seeing the way her pupils dilated and
her lips parted slightly. "It's a date."

Six

In her bathroom at the White Canyon guest ranch two days later, Jillian brushed her hair carefully, a habit she'd developed in the early stages of regrowth. Cody would arrive to pick her up shortly and she was excited about seeing the rodeo together. Excited to see him—far more than she should have been, given their standoff over his granting permission to film on his lands.

Jillian forced herself to set down the hairbrush and quit primping. As much as she admired cancer patients who could bare their bald heads in defiance of the disease, she'd developed a tingling sensitivity in her scalp that had persisted for months. She'd felt cold and naked in so many ways during her treatments, and the lack of hair only added to her sense of being exposed. She'd worn head scarves with abandon, taking inspiration from women of other cultures who kept their heads wrapped. Now, even with the wild curls that covered her skull, she sometimes missed the warmth of the scarves.

Today, however, she would have Cody beside her and that would keep her plenty warm. He wasn't due to arrive for another ten minutes, but as she slid her phone in her purse, she heard the familiar rumble of his voice downstairs.

Was he laughing?

Curious, Jillian slipped from her room and stood beside the heavy wooden railing overlooking the huge foyer below. Madeline McNeill, the proprietor of the White Canyon, sat on the long leather bench in front of the huge windows near the front door. Two other women flanked her; the three of them shared enough physical similarities that they had to be related. They were gathered around an open box full of snowshoes, as the one who seemed the youngest attempted to withdraw her expensive-looking high heel from its snowshoe clamps.

Cody stood with his back to Jillian, facing the women, his good-natured chuckle surprising her.

Until she realized it wasn't Cody at all.

She saw her chance to speak to Carson McNeill personally and hurried downstairs to join them.

"Jillian," Madeline called to her as she entered the foyer. "Do you have a minute? I would like to introduce you to some of the family."

"I'd like that." Her gaze went to Carson first, and it surprised her that a man who looked the same as Cody could be so different.

This one didn't have the same physical effect on her. No warmth, no spark. But his smile was the kind that made you want to smile back, and she did.

"This is my mother," Madeline began, pointing to the older woman in the corner of the window seat. "Paige McNeill."

"Nice to meet you." Jillian stepped forward,

dodging the obstacle course of snowshoes, and squeezed the woman's hand. She couldn't be much older than her midforties, slim and beautiful, with medium honey-colored hair and light green eyes.

"You, too, Jillian." Her gaze skittered away, though her brief smile seemed genuine.

Jillian didn't have long to puzzle over the half-hearted reception before the younger woman sidled up to her. She shared Madeline's long dark hair and blue eyes, but her bangs and curls gave her more of an ingenue look.

"I'm Scarlett, Maddy's sister, and I'm excited to have a movie filmed on McNeill land." She extended her hand, and Jillian saw that her pink-manicured nails were decorated with palm trees. She wore a blue-and-white-polka-dot scarf around her head, a big bow tied behind her hair with the ribbon's ends trailing over one shoulder. "I've already talked Carson into letting a film crew stay at his ranch if Cody doesn't come through for you."

Jillian thought she noticed Paige McNeill frown

before she turned to gaze out the front window. "Cody won't like that," the older woman murmured, mostly to herself, while Scarlett slid a hand around Jillian's elbow and turned her toward Cody's twin.

"This is Carson, the most reasonable of my half brothers."

Jillian reached to shake his hand, but he was holding the aqua-colored high heel shoe he'd helped Scarlett with earlier. He thrust it at his sister and wiped his palm on his jeans before taking Jillian's hand and squeezing it.

"Welcome to Cheyenne, Ms. Jillian. My ranch is all yours whenever you need it."

Jillian thought back to the photos she'd seen of Carson McNeill online and realized she would never confuse him for Cody again. There was a charm about him, for sure—in his pleasing voice and warm smile. Yet having gone through a painful journey herself, she recognized a person battling a deeper hurt, and saw that same starkness in Carson's eyes.

"Thank you. The executives at my company

are really sold on the Black Creek for our project, but if I can persuade them to use your ranch
instead, I will gladly do so." She'd need to make
the decision soon. The shooting location manager and the film's director would touch down
in Cheyenne tomorrow.

"No luck convincing my brother to let you on
his land yet?" Carson asked, while Madeline
stacked up the snowshoes and returned them to
their box.

"No." Jillian felt oddly disloyal talking about
Cody with his family when he wasn't there. "I
understand he has concerns about the potential
dangers."

The room went quiet for an instant. Even Madeline paused briefly in packing up the snowshoes.
Jillian thought she saw a flash of anger, or maybe
hurt, in Carson's gaze. And then it was gone.

"The oldest son is always the responsible one,"
he said drily. "Looks like my twin is here now."
He nodded toward the window. Cody's pickup
truck was pulling into the driveway. "Just keep in

mind my offer. I know the exposure a film could bring would mean a lot to the rest of the family."

He tipped his dark Stetson ever so subtly before stalking toward the kitchen—which was the opposite direction from where his brother was about to enter the room.

Scarlett picked up the theme of the conversation. "We're all really excited about it and flattered you like the area. I read online a little about your company's films. Are you scouting for *Winning the West*?"

"I am." Impressed that Cody's sister had researched the project, Jillian had new appreciation for how valuable an ally the woman might be.

From the window seat, Paige leaned toward them, her honey-colored ponytail falling forward over one shoulder. "You know, Scarlett, not everyone wants to be stuck on a movie set in the middle of nowhere. The actors might be happier if the filming took place in Colorado or someplace closer to LA." She looked to Jillian for support. "I'm sure it must make it easier on the talent to be closer to home. And cheaper."

She seemed so hopeful that Jillian would agree with her; it was obvious Paige wasn't wild about the idea of having a movie crew on her doorstep. Because of the potential dangers Cody had mentioned? Or was there another reason?

Madeline was currently busy taking a phone call, and Scarlett didn't seem to notice her mother's reservations as she scrolled through pages on her phone. "I'm sure they don't care where it's filmed, Mom," she said distractedly. "And it looks like I can get Gramps's pilot to fly me to LA tomorrow, after all, so I'm going to need the day off." Scarlett shot to her feet, her floral skirt swinging around her knees as she headed toward the door.

Cody entered the foyer then, tipping his hat to Scarlett and her mother, who was following fast on her daughter's heels.

"Isn't that kind of sudden?" Paige was saying as they walked away. "If you want to shop, I can go to New York with you…"

The sound of their voices faded as they slipped outside.

Jillian turned her attention to Cody. His broad shoulders filled out his gray Western-cut shirt, and his dark jeans were an upgrade from the work denim she had seen him in last time. His blue eyes lasered in on her and a familiar warmth made her skin tingle.

"Are you ready to rodeo?" he asked, holding out his hand.

The flutter in her belly was an indication of just how ready she was. Now that Carson had offered his ranch for filming, some of the pressure was off. Except the unforgettable views she wanted were still on Cody's land, not his brother's.

And she had the feeling that housing her crew on his twin's property would seem like a betrayal. Maybe tonight, she could change Cody's mind.

"I'm ready." Taking his hand, she gave herself over to at least one more adventure with the rancher who was filling her dreams lately.

Seeing the worry in her eyes, Cody wrapped an arm around Jillian during the last ride of the night. Taking her to the bull-riding finals was sort of like bringing a first date to a scary movie. She gripped his arm every time the chute opened to release another rider into the arena, her fingers squeezing tight while she cheered for every single one of them.

"Did he win?" she asked, when the crowd erupted in cheers after the reigning champ held on for all eight seconds.

Cody chuckled. "It's always a win when you don't end up being dragged by your boot through the dirt. But they're just cheering for his good ride, and because he gets to compete again in the second round of the finals tomorrow."

The dust and the noise rose as the cowboy pumped his fist and the rodeo clowns worked to distract the bull.

"Tomorrow?" She shook her head. "I would think one ride like that in a lifetime was enough." Smiling, she patted her chest. "I don't think I could take the adrenaline spike every day."

"They train hard for this, though. No one ends up riding a bull unless they love the sport." Cody led her out of their row of seats, wanting to show her more of Frontier Days than just the rodeo. There was a whole carnival waiting outside, with live music and plenty of attractions. "Carson competed for a long time until he broke so many bones our father threatened to give Creek Spill to someone else unless Carson quit the sport."

"And that worked?" Jillian frowned, glancing up at Cody. "I only met him briefly, but he didn't strike me as the kind of man who would respond well to an ultimatum."

"He didn't. But by the time he was healed up and ready to start training again, his fiancée left him for another guy on the tour. Carson decided it wasn't worth circulating in that world again."

"How awful." She took Cody's hand as they wound their way out of the arena. The temperature outside had dropped, but was still mild.

Midway lights flashed red, green and blue in every direction and a big wooden ride on a pendulum swooshed past them overhead. The scents of funnel cakes and hot turkey legs was heavy in the air.

"Though it may have saved Carson from hurting himself even more. I think he's got screws holding him together."

"Still, it has to hurt to see a dream die like that." She wrapped her arms around herself.

"Sooner or later, he would have had to come home and face the reality of running the family business anyhow." Cody had pulled his brother's weight for too long as it was. He rubbed a hand along Jillian's back, feeling the delicate curve at the base of her spine. "Are you warm enough?"

"I'm fine." She nodded, but she looked chilled. "I don't think that pursuing a dream means you're not facing reality. Some people might argue that our dreams are the most important reality we have. They anchor us and make life worth living."

He'd touched a nerve. "It's different for Carson."

"Because he's not a cancer survivor?" she quickly retorted. "That doesn't make his dreams any less important."

"Wait." Cody drew a deep breath and hoped she would, too. "I didn't mean to suggest that.

Selfishly, I'm glad Carson's focus is back on our business. And for his sake, I'm relieved he's still in one piece, because you saw how dangerous bull riding can be."

She nodded stiffly, accepting his answer.

"I know my parents aren't supportive of my new direction in life, because they perceive it as irresponsible. So I can't help but empathize with your brother." She rubbed a hand along her arm again. "And I am getting a little chilly."

He nodded, looking up and down the midway at the shops, grateful for the change of subject. "Let's keep walking." He picked up the pace.

"Sometimes I think being cold is psychosomatic. You know what it's like when you wake up from surgery and the drugs are making you cold?" She glanced up at him as they neared the vendors showing their wares. "They slow your heart rate or something? It's like that, where I feel like I'm chilled on the inside."

He imagined that her surgeries to remove tumors had been scarier than most, especially with the added fear that they might not be able to excise all the cancer. He hated that she'd been through that. Hated that he couldn't do anything to change the past for her. But he could do one thing for her now, at least. Looking around the carnival, Cody spotted what he needed. He led her toward a big, well-lit display from a local Western clothing supplier. He brought her to the women's flannel shirts and held up a red one.

Smiling, she looked down at herself with the shirt in front of her. "Doesn't it clash with my hair?"

"I like you in bright colors." He enjoyed seeing the vivid splash of hues all around this vibrant woman. He grabbed another one, which was purple and blue. "How about this?"

He could tell by her expression she liked it. There was a little flicker of interest in her eyes, maybe. He wondered when he'd started to notice those small details about her.

"Purple is more me," she admitted, unbuttoning it to try it on. She went to a full-length mirror hanging on one of the posts holding up the display and slid her arms into the sleeves. The shirt fit perfectly.

Cody popped off the tag and gave it to a hovering saleswoman in a crisp white Stetson.

"I can get it," Jillian protested. "I want to pay my own way."

"Not a chance. You're my guest." He passed over the cash and told the woman to keep the change. Then he returned to Jillian's side and watched as she buttoned up the shirt. "If you want the full rodeo experience, you need a souvenir."

"The full rodeo experience?" Smoothing the collar down to her satisfaction, she turned from the mirror and faced him. "In that case, thank you."

Her hazel eyes were more gold tonight, reflecting the lights of the carnival midway. He couldn't deny the pull of attraction, the desire to get closer to her. Their fast and furious time together in his office Friday night hadn't eased his need for her in the least. Now there was a new element to his feelings for her, too. The urge to protect her.

"We're not done yet." His gaze dipped to her lips, and he remembered how she tasted.

"We're not?" Her voice softened as her eyes locked on his.

Even more than he wanted to kiss her, he wanted to shield her from any more blows life tried to deal her. To make her smile.

"Not by half." He lowered his head to speak into her ear, inhaling the scent of her hair. "It's not a rodeo without a turkey leg."

Two hours later, Jillian looked out the passenger-side window of Cody's pickup truck, warmed by her new flannel shirt and the cowboy in the driver's seat. She hadn't necessarily expected to share the adventures from her list with another person, but she had to admit that attending the rodeo with Cody McNeill had been fun. She'd tasted the funnel cake, a turkey leg and even a few bites of a caramel apple that had been out of this world.

Or maybe everything had tasted delectable because of the company she kept. Because she'd been thinking about kissing him every time he offered her a bite.

Now, as the truck rumbled up the long driveway of the White Canyon guest ranch, she wondered how the night would end. She knew they couldn't take things any further than the front seat of his truck would allow. Not with his half sister watching over the foyer.

Of course, Jillian couldn't allow their attraction to sway her into making another bad decision, anyhow. She had thought a night with him sounded sexy and exciting when she was thinking solely of her life adventures and how much this man reawakened her senses. But that had been before she knew him better. Before she realized how much "adventure" was out of character for this fiercely practical, responsible rancher.

He wouldn't be kissing her senseless again anytime soon. Not when he viewed their encounter at Wrangler's as a deception on her part. After all, he'd accused her of trying to circumvent him by seducing his "twin."

"Everything okay?" he asked her as he pulled

up to the White Canyon. "You've been quiet the whole ride home."

He parked the truck and pocketed the keys. Landscaping lights around a few prominent cottonwoods illuminated the walkway to the wide front stairs of the guest ranch.

"Just thinking about what's next," she admitted, shifting to see him better as she slid off her seat belt. "Debating if I should give up asking you to film at the Black Creek or—"

"Yes," he told her flatly. "That's not happening."

Frustration that he hadn't even given her a chance to get out the rest of her proposal and plead her case simmered.

"Then you should know your brother already offered to house the production crew at the Creek Spill." She didn't even realize she'd made up her mind to accept that offer until she heard the words roll off her tongue. But what choice did Cody give her?

She'd have to find a way to talk the film executives into the alternate location.

"You already spoke to Carson about this?" His blue eyes narrowed as he stared at her from across the dim truck cab. "Without telling me?"

"You knew I was interested in filming up here," she reminded him. "And that I had planned to speak to Carson at some point—"

"I remember you were plotting to intercept Carson all along. Even before I landed in your path Friday and confused things." His jaw flexed and a shadow crossed his expression. "I imagine my twin was very accommodating."

She didn't appreciate his implication or his tone, since she wasn't the kind of woman to pit brother against brother. Yet even through the crackle of frustration, she felt the pull of this man in the small, enclosed space. Remembered the way it had felt to be pressed against him, peeling off each other's clothes. To distract herself from those thoughts, she stared out at the night sky full of stars.

"Scarlett approached him before I did. Apparently, she thinks a film shot here will boost the profile of the other McNeill businesses besides ranching."

"Of course she does. She met an actor on a flight to LA a few months ago and it reignited her old hope of trying her luck in Hollywood." Cody shifted in his seat, his voice a rumble that vibrated through her. "I'm sure she sees a film in Cheyenne as a way to brighten up her otherwise boring life. She's a typical twenty-five-year-old."

Jillian told herself this wasn't her family and she had no reason to weigh in with her opinion. But in light of her own journey, she found it too hard to keep her feelings to herself. She was probably more let down than she should have been that a man who attracted her so much could feel that way.

"Maybe Scarlett's already seen the way your brother lost out on his bull-riding dream, and she doesn't want to become the next McNeill to sacrifice her future to the good of the ranch." Levering the truck door open, Jillian didn't wait for Cody to help her out. "Not everyone wants to spend their whole life playing it safe."

She shouldn't want a man like Cody—someone so bound to an idea of what was right that he couldn't appreciate the idea of being happy. Before he could argue with her anymore, she said a terse thank-you and good-night, and exited the truck.

Only to have him catch up to her halfway up the walkway. He matched her fast gait, opening the door to the guest ranch for her.

"Who says I want to play it safe?" He stared down at her in the porch light, his gaze intense.

Missing nothing.

She'd stopped too close to him. The nearness of his body communicated a whole different set of messages than the conversation they'd been having.

Attraction. Hunger. Desire.

"When it comes to the film—" she struggled to keep a thought in her head as she glanced up at him, breathing in the warm hint of spice from his aftershave, a scent she could almost taste on her tongue in her memories "—you won't risk anyone's safety."

"Correct." He somehow managed to hold the screen door open for her while simultaneously blocking the threshold, his broad shoulders taking up all the room. "I won't risk anyone else's safety. But that doesn't mean I won't consider a gamble of my own."

Her mouth was too dry for conversation. All she really wanted was a kiss. To lose herself in this man. It made no logical sense, since she was frustrated with him and all the ways he was thwarting her career. But she couldn't deny the heavy pulse of blood in her veins. The tingle of anticipation on her skin.

"I don't understand." She shook her head, her hair teasing her oversensitive skin as it brushed her cheek and bare collarbone. "You aren't gambling a damn thing."

Her voice sounded breathless. She felt light-headed.

He backed her up a step, letting the screen door close behind him as he slid his hands around her waist. The sensual impact of that touch flared hot inside her.

"On the contrary." He leaned closer, his lips hovering just above hers. His voice got softer as he breathed the words over her mouth. "I risk my sanity every time I'm next to you, Jillian."

Seven

You're insane.

Scarlett reread her sister Maisie's text as she packed her suitcase for the trip to Los Angeles.

Her flight had been easy to arrange on short notice. It helped that her grandfather had a private plane, a Learjet that he had made available to her, since no one else in the family needed it for the next few days. Her father had tried to warn her that Malcolm McNeill was only attempting to buy her affection, but Scarlett didn't think that was the case. She'd been spending afternoons with her grandfather and his new girlfriend, Rose, learning more about the rest of the family that her father had turned his back on before she was born. Scarlett had met a few of her cousins, including Gabe McNeill, the youngest son of Donovan's brother, Liam. Scarlett had even flown to Martinique this winter to spend some time with Gabe and his new wife, Brianne.

That trip had brought her closer to the rest of the family, including Rose, a feisty former singer in her eighties, who was Brianne's grandmother. Malcolm treated Rose like royalty, but not just by spending money on her. Yes, he'd bought himself and Rose matching, high-end smartphones, but just so they could download all the apps their family members used and figure them out together over a pot of tea in the afternoon.

It was adorable. Unlike Maisie's texts.

Why insane?? Scarlett texted back, as she studied the contents of her wardrobe critically. Because I'm doing something I want to do instead of what the family expects??

She didn't have to wait long for Maisie's reply.

Because you're surprising him. He ghosted you last year, babe. What makes you think he's going to be happy to see you now?

Scarlett's stomach twisted. It was her own fault for sharing that private pain with her sister in a moment of weakness. She should have never confessed that story to Maisie, of all people, who'd never doubted herself for an instant.

I don't care if he's happy. I plan to tell him in no uncertain terms what I think of him.

Of course, Logan might not be pleased to see her. But even worse was the fear that he might not remember her at all. Scarlett's worst nightmare was being forgettable, a fear her older sisters would never understand. Madeline and Maisie were born secure. They were both smart and beautiful, and had received full-ride scholarships to top-tier universities. They shared the McNeill good looks. And, most important, their father acknowledged them, appreciated their contributions to the family businesses in his own gruff way.

Scarlett looked like their mother—pretty in a way that would fade over time, her beauty a fiction created by silk and bows, accessories and makeup. She was the daughter her mother had wanted and her father hadn't. The baby. The "one too many," according to whispered arguments she'd overheard as a child.

Not that it mattered anymore. Scarlett had stuck around Cheyenne after college more for her mother's sake than to honor her dad's insistence she give something back to the family. Her mom had been deeply unhappy for years, and Scarlett felt no one else noticed.

Perhaps that was why she so fully identified with her mother. No one would notice Scarlett either if she didn't make the effort every day to rise above her average looks. To paint a cat's eye on her lids and swirl glitter in the shadow she used under her brow bone.

Sifting through the outfits of every color in her wardrobe, Scarlett pulled out a dress raided from

Madeline's closet long ago, a gold lace stunner from the Halloween when Maddy had dressed as a flapper. Scarlett could picture the fringed hem going well with white leather go-go boots and her dark hair piled on her head in a modified beehive.

She might not be beautiful, but she knew how to look hot.

She was packing the outfit in tissue paper for her trip when her phone chimed again.

That's more like it. Want some backup?

Scarlett felt tempted. But how much satisfaction could she take in her big moment if she needed her sister to hold her hand? No. Better to tell him off on her own.

Steeling herself, she texted back, I've got this, and slid her cell phone into her purse.

Scarlett swallowed her fears and zipped up her overnight bag for tomorrow's trip. She wasn't settling for being the also-ran McNeill anymore.

She would go to LA and finally step out of the shadows of her successful family members.

And make Logan King eat his sorry heart out.

Kissing Jillian tonight had not been in Cody's plan.

He'd intended only to keep her close for a few more days until he could convince her to get a blood test. After the mishap with the condom, he needed to rule out any chance of pregnancy. Then she'd leave town for good, especially now that his brother had interfered and offered Creek Spill for the filming. Her work was almost done here.

But being with her made Cody want her again. Simple as that. The attraction was as automatic as breathing, happening on its own whether he willed it or not. He could tell the same was true for her, because she'd stormed out of his truck a minute ago and now here they were, inches apart on the front porch of the White Canyon Ranch, unable to keep their hands off each other.

She reached for his face, her fingers trailing

down his cheek and along his jaw, her green eyes following the movement before her gaze tracked back to his.

He bent to kiss her, a barely there graze of his lips over hers. She tasted like funnel cake sugar, so sweet he wanted a lick. He took in the feel of her as she wound her arms around his neck, her whole body swaying against him.

"This is crazy," she whispered, as a night breeze blew around them and she pressed closer. "We can't get carried away out here where anyone can see us."

"You're right." Taking her hand in his, he pivoted, drawing her toward the back of the building. "I know a better place."

He didn't want to go in through the front door and risk running into Madeline or any guests who might try to draw them into conversation. He wanted Jillian all to himself. He guided her down one side of the wraparound porch to steps that led into a rose garden.

"Wait." She halted on the flagstone path between two towering rosebushes, their scent heavy even in the cool evening air. "Why continue this madness? You can't get me out of Wyoming fast enough, but you're willing to sneak me into my hotel up the back stairs so we can..." She shook her head, unwilling to complete the thought.

Cody kept hold of her hand, feeling her pulse throb fast at the base of her palm. A soft, subtle hint of how he affected her.

"Who said I want you to leave? Just because I'm in no hurry to have a movie crew film on my ranch doesn't mean I want you to go." He liked the idea of Jillian sticking around. For one thing, he hoped she'd stay at least until he could convince her to get the blood test. For another? He wasn't done exploring this attraction. How long could a powerful draw like this last?

He needed to know. And intended to find out with her.

Her eyes searched his. "You mean I've been misreading all your cues? Like when you accused me of plotting to intercept your brother on the night we met?" She arched an eyebrow. "I took that as a sign you weren't pleased about me being in Cheyenne."

The breeze rumpled her curls, which softened the scowl on her face.

Cody wanted to kiss them away from her mouth. To feel the strands of hair on his bare skin. For now, he skimmed them off her cheek.

"You should have read it as a sign that I don't want you to ever look at my brother the way you look at me." He could burn himself on that heated gaze of hers. "Because that's all it meant."

Her mouth worked silently for a moment, then snapped shut.

"And I'm not trying to sneak you up the back stairs to your room right now," he added, remembering the other accusation she'd lobbed at him.

"You're not?" She glanced up at the building.

"No." He leaned closer to speak into her ear. "If you're interested in a little more privacy, I thought you might like seeing The Villa."

A slow smile spread over her face. "There's a villa nearby?" She turned her head back and forth, looking in both directions. "On the grounds of a Wyoming guest ranch?"

"'The Villa' is what we call the only freestanding unit for guests. It's more of a bungalow, but in the literature for this place, my sister labeled it that." Cody led Jillian through the rose garden to the far edge of the grounds. "Apparently, the name helps communicate the level of luxury. It doesn't get rented very often."

"No one's staying there now?" Jillian asked as they arrived at the building in question and stepped onto the lit front porch. In most of its details, The Villa mirrored the look of the main house.

"I am." He took out his master key card printed with the White Canyon logo and passed it to her. "I reserved it just in case."

Her slender fingers wrapped around the key and she stared down at it.

"Just in case…" She flicked the plastic against her nails. "You thought there might be a vicious storm tonight that would prevent you from driving the rest of the way home?"

He shrugged. "That particular scenario didn't occur to me. No."

"I have a perfectly good room upstairs in the main house," she reminded him, settling the edge of the key card on his chest before lightly dragging it down the front of him. "Just in case you suddenly wanted somewhere to stay."

"I wouldn't want the rest of the ranch guests speculating about us if I followed you up those main stairs." He wanted Jillian all to himself. All night long.

He didn't want to spare an extra second of his time fielding questions about how their evening went.

"I don't care what anyone else thinks." Her eyes were serious for a moment, as her hands hovered at his waist. "I let go of worries like that two years ago."

When she'd been treated for cancer. His chest constricted as he thought about her battling for her life.

"I had another reason for wanting this space." He'd messaged the housekeeper from the rodeo to ensure the room was readied the way he wanted. "But only if you're game."

"You know I can't say no to an adventure." Jillian held up the card and moved toward the door.

She slid the plastic into the lock mechanism and the light turned green. He opened the door.

Heat rushed out from the room; the hearth glowed with a freshly laid fire. The scent of applewood and hickory filled the air.

"I thought you might appreciate the warmth of a fire," he said, following her into the room after locking the door behind them. Then he saw the expression on her face.

The naked emotion.

And—damn it to hell. The tear.

Cody McNeill was supposed to be her adventure.

Her wild fling that helped resurrect her long-snoozing sensuality.

He was not supposed to touch her heart with a tenderness that brought her to her knees.

Blinking from the brightness of the fire, Jillian

tried to swallow back the sudden tide of emotions threatening to swamp her. She didn't want Cody to see how his kindness affected her. Couldn't bear to expose another piece of her soul.

But when she pivoted on her heel to face him, she could see his hesitation. His careful consideration of her reaction, as though she were a puzzle to solve rather than a sensual woman. By letting her runaway emotions intrude, she'd ruined the mood just when things were getting heated.

So, unwilling to deal with any of it, unable to let her cancer steal this from her, Jillian tossed the key card on the floor and headed toward Cody. She ignored the question in his eyes and flung her arms around his neck.

Then she kissed him like it was her last night on earth.

And his, too.

She worked the fastenings on his shirt with unsteady hands, attraction and emotion fueled by a new frenzy. She craved having his caresses all over her, hot and possessive, to see if this chemistry was as combustible as she remembered. To burn away the tangle of confused feelings until all that was left was passion.

"Jillian." Cody broke the kiss long enough to rasp her name, his chest rising and falling like he'd run a marathon.

Meeting his gaze in the glow of orange firelight, she paused long enough to see what he wanted.

"Are you sure?" His fingers traced a path down one cheek before he tipped her chin up. "About this?"

Her grip tightened on the cotton shirttails she'd dragged from his jeans, the fabric still warm in her hands. "This might be the only thing in the whole world that I'm positive about right now."

His eyes lingered on her for a moment—long enough that she wondered what he saw. A woman desperate to feel desirable? Whole? But no matter. Because a moment later, he nodded. Decision made.

"Come with me." He took her hand and led her into the darker recesses of the guesthouse.

They went through a cool kitchen, where the

only light was the glint of the fire reflecting off stainless steel appliances, and past a staircase with a heavy pine banister. They finally arrived at an open door toward the back of the unit. More flickering light emanated from within.

The master bedroom, she realized. There was another fire laid in the simple black hearth. The glow illuminated a king-size sleigh bed with a simple white duvet and a mountain of white pillows in every size. A tea cart near the bed held a white ceramic pitcher, stemware and a few silver-domed platters.

A pewter cup held a bouquet of echinacea flowers in yellow, red and purple.

While she took it all in, Cody drew her forward, deeper into the room that had been so carefully prepared for them.

"You should have a bed this time," he told her simply, explaining his thoughtfulness. "Every time."

He stopped at the edge of the footboard, hooking a finger in her flannel shirt to tug her one step closer. Until there was only a breath between them.

He was so near, and yet it felt like she was standing at the edge of a cliff. Like if she moved forward that fraction of an inch, she would be in free fall, tumbling down into something deep and unknown.

"I'm so ready for this." She said it aloud. To herself. To him.

She didn't know if it was true. But she wanted to lose herself in his touch. His hands.

His answer was a kiss on her cheek. Impossibly gentle, but the start of so much more. She tipped her head back, giving him everything. All of her.

He kissed his way to her ear. Her neck. Down her throat. He undid the rest of the buttons on her shirt, sliding the flannel apart. Tugging the gauzy blouse over her head. Flicking free the clasp of a bra that hid the rumpled knot of scars on one breast.

Last time they were together had been so rushed, so hungry, that she'd never been naked. Never had to worry about the roped surgery marks where the surgeons had operated to remove her tumor, or the patches of pink, shiny skin from radiation therapy.

Threading her fingers through his, she gently steered him away from her breasts, wanting to prepare him.

"My body is…" She blinked, not ready to have this conversation. Not sure how she even felt about her scars. "I just don't want you to be surprised. I'm a little…misshapen."

She didn't feel ashamed, necessarily. She felt proud of her body for surviving. For triumphing.

But at this moment, she wished it was beautiful.

"You're exactly the right shape for a warrior. A survivor. I can't imagine anything more beautiful." His gaze was steady. "Does it bother you to be touched there?"

His words soothed her. Eased her doubts.

"No." She shook her head, a curl grazing her cheek. "It feels good."

"Then I hope you'll let me touch you more." He eased his fingers free from where she'd held him back. "But first I'm going to lay you right in the middle of all those pillows."

His hands spanned her waist and he lifted her. She held on to his shoulders until he dropped her gently in the center of the bed. The cream-colored lace of her bra still fluttered open around her chest, the straps loose on her shoulders.

Cody tugged off her boots and her jeans, setting them aside before he stripped naked. The fire-light burnished his skin with a bronze glow. His muscles rippled as he moved: the thick, corded ones in his back, the flat, taut ones of his abs. Her throat went dry as she looked at him.

Then he was with her, using his weight to shift her on the bed as he stretched out. He rested one warm palm on her belly, steadying her while he kissed her throat. Her collarbone. Lower.

She told herself not to worry, but that didn't stop her from tensing when he dragged a thumb along one thick line of scars. Or when he stroked the pink expanse from the radiation burn.

"Your body is a miracle," he whispered over

her skin before he licked a path around her nipple, then sucked gently.

Desire flooded through her, hot and fast, drowning her insecurity in a pool of want. By the time he switched his attention to her other breast, she was so distracted by the heat between her thighs she forgot about anything else.

Jillian snaked her leg around his, holding him against her, rocking her hips into his. She wanted more. Now. The ache of waiting coiled tight inside her.

Fingers flexing against his shoulders, she closed her eyes. She knew she wouldn't last long. Not when the tension was mounting every minute.

He slipped a hand between her legs, touching her just where she needed. The pleasure came so hard and fast she shuddered with it, experiencing waves of sweet, tender release. Clinging to him, she let it roll over her. Through her. When the last spasm hit her, she opened her eyes for a moment—just long enough to see him roll a condom in place.

She unwound her arms and legs from him

enough that he could move on top of her and position himself between her thighs. Enter her inch by tantalizing inch.

Raining kisses on his chest, his neck, wherever she could reach, Jillian moved with him, wanting him to feel every bit as fulfilled as she already did. The scent of his aftershave, the taste of his skin, burned into her brain a searing memory she'd never forget. She gave herself over to the joining, back arching so he could capture the taut peak of one breast and then the other again. The feel of his tongue there, loving her body where it had been hurt and neglected for so long, was a potent kind of alchemy.

It changed her somehow. Changed how she felt about her body and sex, so that it all seemed unbearably beautiful. Another orgasm built inside her. When it charged through her, she felt it in every nerve ending, all the way to her toes. She held him tight, and his body tensed before a final thrust put him over the edge in turn.

By then, as the last aftershock faded, Jillian was speechless. Awed. Something wonderful had happened for her. A new acceptance of herself. A new joy in her beleaguered body. And this responsible, practical man of few words had wrought that magic with his hands and his quiet tenderness.

It wasn't supposed to happen this way. Not that she regretted this time with him. But she wasn't ready to have the earth moved and her reality shifted by any man. She had a list of adventures to experience and a promise to herself she would not break.

But with her heart already dancing dizzy pirouettes after their charged encounter, Jillian knew she needed space fast. Distance. She rolled away from him while they each caught their breath.

"Cody—"

"Jillian—"

They started talking at the same time.

"You go first," she offered, not even sure what she would have said. How would she tell him that she needed to get back to LA? That she couldn't afford to stick around Cheyenne and fall for a hot rancher with magic in his hands?

"I have a favor to ask." He reached behind her to drag the duvet around her so she was covered. Warm.

"And how clever of you to ask it when I'm swamped with endorphins and still reeling with physical bliss." She tucked the blanket closer to her chin, rolling over to look in his eyes.

His very serious eyes.

It occurred to her too late that Cody might be concocting a plan to give himself space and distance at the same time she was. Her stomach tightened into a knot.

"You've already gotten my brother's okay to film on his land, and I know that means I could wake up any day and find you gone." He brushed her hair from her face, his touch making her pulse flutter even now.

"I have to show the executives from my company around first. Make sure they're okay with using his ranch instead of the one we really want—Black Creek." She wondered if he would ever budge on that issue.

"I understand." He nodded, but didn't offer his

ranch. "Before you leave Cheyenne, I want you to consider having a blood test."

His words hung in the air between them. Jarring.

She hadn't been expecting anything like that. Hadn't realized he was already making a plan for his life once she was gone.

"A blood test." She repeated the words, unable to make the idea reconcile with what they'd just shared. With everything she'd been feeling.

"Yes. A blood test is sensitive enough to detect pregnancy this early." The reasonable, practical Cody reasserted himself. "I think we'll both sleep better once we rule out any chance you've conceived."

The bubble of sensual euphoria burst. At least, she hoped that was the only thing breaking inside her. Because his statement rattled the hell out of her.

A chill crept over her despite the blaze roaring in the hearth at the foot of the bed.

"Of course." She straightened, letting the duvet fall away as she searched for her shirt. "If you'll make the appointment, I'll show up." After punching her fists through the armholes of her blouse, she fastened the bra clasp under the fabric, since the straps were still perched on her shoulders. "I wouldn't want you to lose sleep."

He sat the rest of the way up in bed. "Wait a second. Where are you—"

"I'm sorry. I forgot that one of my bosses is flying in first thing tomorrow." She slid on her jeans and stepped into her boots. "I can't afford to screw up anything else on this job."

Grabbing her purse, she headed for the door.

Eight

After finishing up a meeting with his foreman the following Monday, Cody stalked out of the Black Creek Ranch office. Next month, once renovations were complete, he would move more of the business side of the ranch work to his new facility in town.

A location that would be forever associated in his mind with his passionate first encounter with Jillian.

But for now, Cody's business manager still worked out of an old double-bay garage that had been converted to office space over a decade ago.

Jamming his hat on his head in deference to the noontime sun, Cody headed toward his truck. He needed to get to Cheyenne for the appointment he'd made for Jillian to have a blood test. He'd wanted to drive her there personally, since he hadn't seen her in days—not so much as a glimpse of her after she'd walked out on him at the White Canyon. He'd received a text message in which she'd politely refused his offer of a ride, although she'd agreed to meet him at the assigned appointment time.

Her continued distance stung more than it should have. More even than her walking out on him last week. Clearly, she needed space, something he understood well, since he was the kind of man who needed plenty of space of his own. Yet he'd assumed she would speak to him again. Explain why she'd felt compelled to sprint out the door after the most powerful physical encounter of his life. He knew he hadn't been alone in feeling that way. She'd been right there with him.

Until she wasn't.

He didn't know what he'd done wrong, but after

the blood test, he would speak to her. Clear the air and, he hoped, convince her that she didn't need to rush out of town the moment the results came back. How could she ignore the attraction that pulled at him day and night, on his mind even when Jillian was nowhere in sight?

He'd almost reached the truck when he heard the rumble of a four-wheeler coming from the west pasture. Turning, he saw the familiar figure of his father riding toward him.

Cody pocketed his keys and checked the time on his phone. He had a few minutes to spare before he needed to leave. Lifting a hand in greeting, he started toward his dad. A tractor hummed in the distance, haying one of the north fields.

Donovan McNeill had tried his best the last few years to let his sons take over the ranching operations, but Cody knew it wasn't easy for the older man to give up the reins completely. And truth be told, he appreciated his father's input. Whereas his twin butted heads with Donovan often, Cody's opinions usually aligned with his dad's.

Donovan straightened in the seat as he pulled

to a halt and switched off the machine, a cloud of dust spinning around them both. At six feet, he was shorter than his sons, but he shared similar features, including the straight nose and strong jaw. The heavy eyebrows and blue eyes. Even the girls took after him, except for Scarlett, who'd inherited the softer features of her mother.

"You know about this production company that wants to film on our land?" his father began without preamble, as if they'd been in the middle of a conversation.

He didn't look happy. Still, he reached out to pet Morticia when the border collie bounded over to greet him.

"I'm aware. I refused them permission." Cody understood his father would be resistant—he'd never appreciated strangers on McNeill property.

"Then you're also aware that your brother is allowing the whole thing to happen at the Creek Spill?"

"The rest of the family backs him." No surprise there. Carson had been born with a knack for rallying others around him. He'd been the crowd favorite every time he saddled up in their rodeo days.

"Not me. And not Paige." The older man's jaw flexed as he stared out toward the north field, where the haying operation produced a steady mechanical hum. "Your siblings are already flocking around my father like he's the second coming, even though I told them that he's oily as a snake. Now this?" He shook his head. "I'm still a part of this family, damn it."

Cody had known Donovan wouldn't approve of outsiders tromping around the property, but it surprised him that his wife was against the idea, too.

"Paige doesn't want the film crew here?" His stepmother was a quiet woman. She taught yoga classes in town and spent long hours baking, sending healthy, homemade treats to soup kitchens, family and friends. She'd been a good mother to him after his own had died.

Still, she'd never been "Mom." Not to him and not to his brothers. She'd been their babysitter first. Even after she married their father, she'd always been Paige.

"She's adamantly opposed." His father frowned, the lines in his face settling in a natural scowl, as if the unhappiness had long been carved there. "I think she's worried about Scarlett." He shook his head as if that didn't quite add up. "Maybe she's afraid once our baby girl gets a taste of the movie business, she'll leave here for good."

"Scarlett's a grown woman," Cody replied, wondering why Paige would be so upset. She'd never been opposed to much of anything before—let alone adamantly. Her oft-repeated mantra was live and let live.

"You know she left town last week for a trip to the West Coast? She might already be making plans for a move."

Cody hadn't been pleased that she would just drop her responsibilities at the ranch and take off, but she'd hired a temp worker to fill in for her.

"Just because she's a grown woman doesn't mean she's going to make a good decision," Donovan grumbled. "Either way, I know it would mean a lot to your stepmother if we can shut this thing down. I woke up last night and found her doing internet searches for airfare to New Zealand."

"She wants to take a trip?" Cody had never known her to leave Wyoming, let alone the continental United States.

"I'm not sure." His father crossed his arms and knitted his brows. He was troubled, no doubt about it. "She said she's been considering an anniversary trip for us, since we never took a honeymoon."

"Sounds reasonable for a landmark twenty-fifth celebration." The answer seemed clear enough to Cody. Paige was long overdue for a vacation.

"She's never been one for traveling outside the state, let alone across the globe," Donovan growled. "Something doesn't sit right and I don't know what to believe. Just…" He waved at the air, a frustrated gesture, before leaning forward to switch on the ignition of the four-wheeler.

"See what you can do." Then he roared off in a
new cloud of dust.

Cody pulled his keys from his pocket and
stalked to his truck; he didn't want to be late
meeting Jillian at the doctor's office. He couldn't
puzzle out what was going on in his family. Especially Scarlett's hunger to leave Cheyenne behind and his twin's insistence on opening up the
ranch to Hollywood and all the inconveniences
and possible dangers sure to come with it.

And now his father and stepmother seemed
to be having problems. Problems rooted in that
damn movie. The McNeills had been struggling
with the reentry of their grandfather in their lives
even before Paige started acting funny. But now,
with all the stress the film added to the mix, he
feared his family was fracturing at the seams.

He had Jillian to thank for that. Not that he
would have minded so much if she'd been willing to stick around for the aftermath. To see the
project through while his family contended with
all the changes it wrought. Instead, she seemed

content to turn her back on all of them and pro-
ceed onto her next adventure.

Forgetting about him and the incredible time
they'd spent together.

Jillian was awaiting her test results at the doctor's office when Cody arrived. He crossed the
reception area in no time, his long strides eating
up the small space between them.

He dropped his black Stetson on a nearby chair
and sat down on the seat beside her. As if they
were lovers on good terms instead of…whatever
they were.

She hadn't seen him in days. Five and a half,
to be exact. Not that she'd expected him to
chase after her when she'd left the bungalow at
the White Canyon Ranch. But maybe she'd expected more from him after their time together
at the rodeo. Their time together afterward. He'd
said he wanted to share adventures with her. The
rodeo date *had* been his idea.

They hadn't been able to keep their hands off
each other. But then after their lovemaking, his

primary concern had been obtaining a blood test to assure himself she couldn't possibly be carrying his child. That cold realization had been upsetting to her. It had killed the passion of the moment.

"They've already drawn my blood," she informed him, hoping she sounded detached and indifferent. She would not let him see that he'd hurt her. "The nurse said she could have the results for us in one hour, so I assumed you would want to wait."

"I do." He wore dark jeans and a black button-down shirt that stretched taut across his shoulders when he leaned forward to flip idly through the magazines on the coffee table. Every one of the publications featured a baby or a pregnant woman. He sat back in the seat again, empty-handed. "And I'm sorry I'm late. My father paid me a visit just as I was ready to get in my truck. He rarely needs to talk about anything, so I found it tough to cut things short."

Some of her irritation eased as she imagined a man even quieter than the brooding cowboy next to her. Donovan McNeill must surely be the strong, silent type. Jillian would rather think about the McNeill men right now than stare at those magazines full of babies she might never have—even with her frozen eggs. And she felt that aching emptiness each time a wriggling baby or pregnant mother passed through the obstetrician's waiting area.

"It's fine." Jillian had planned to use their time before they got the results to gauge where she stood with Cody. She thought it was only fair to tell him when the film would start shooting, since her boss had agreed to her plan B for location shots on *Winning the West*. Now, she only needed to file applications for a few more permits and she could start looking at weather forecasts to ensure the crew arrived on-site at the best time.

What would that mean for her and Cody? Once her job here was over, should she avoid returning to Cheyenne? Was this blood test his way of cutting ties with her?

She glanced at him cautiously. There was a

furrow of concern between his brows, and he seemed distracted. At the moment, the waiting area was empty except for the two of them, the big clock on the wall ticking audibly over a children's play area.

"Is everything okay with your family? I hope your father didn't have bad news."

"He's worried about Scarlett. And my stepmother, apparently." Cody turned his gaze to Jillian. She noticed his hand clenching on his knee. "The film shoot has Paige upset and he's not sure why."

Jillian fidgeted with the denim strap of her purse. "I remember the night before the rodeo, when I met Paige, she did seem worried about it. And she definitely didn't want Scarlett to go to LA."

"That's what my dad said." Cody appeared to mull it over. "But I think there's something else going on. Possibly some problems between him and Paige."

"I'm sorry to hear that." Jillian hadn't intended to stir up trouble for the McNeills. "But your siblings are excited for this opportunity, and my company has committed to shooting here. It's happening."

That got his full attention. "Just like that?"

"I spent two days showing my boss around the Creek Spill." She'd been forthright with Cody about this from the start, so she didn't intend to feel guilty now. "She convinced the director that this is the right spot."

The muscle in his jaw flexed. Because he was angry with her? Or with his brother for not siding with him?

She didn't have time to ask as a nurse called her name. "Jillian? The doctor will see you now."

In a flash, her train of thought did a one-eighty. She knew what the doctor would say, and that this visit was a simple formality. It was the last thread tying her and Cody together, one he was all too glad to break. Memories of their last night together—the way it had pulled at her heart and, by contrast, the way he had been able to enjoy the physical release simply for its own sake—forced her to be a realist.

After today, she would have no reason to stay in Cheyenne. The location manager would take over, releasing Jillian from any more work on the site.

Oddly numb, she braced herself for the expected news as she entered the office. Dr. Simmons, a woman of about sixty with long, graying braids, stood to shake hands with both of them before flipping open the file folder on her small oak desk. While she reviewed the papers, Jillian's eye went to the front of the desk, which was completely covered with children's artwork—everything from finger-paint hearts to scribbled coloring book pages.

"It appears I have good news for you." The doctor smiled as she lifted the first sheet out of the file and passed it to Jillian. "Congratulations to you both. You're pregnant, Ms. Ross."

Jillian couldn't take the paper. Couldn't process what she was hearing. Vaguely, she noticed Cody sit forward in his chair beside her.

"Excuse me?" she asked, her voice scratchy and hoarse.

"May I?" Cody reached for the page of test results, since Jillian still couldn't make her hand move.

"The blood test confirms that you're expecting," Dr. Simmons explained, her small brown eyes staying focused on Jillian even as she passed the paper to Cody. "The test is very definitive. Your pregnancy hormone levels are well above normal."

Stunned, Jillian couldn't wrap her brain around the words. Or maybe she was too terrified to do so.

"But I've had cancer." She shook her head, remembering all the things they'd done to her body. All the poisons they'd flooded her with to kill the tumor. She couldn't possibly be pregnant now. "Radiation. Chemo."

She felt Cody's hand on her back. Rubbing. Comforting. He was scanning the results even as he tugged her closer. She couldn't get a full breath of air, her chest constricting.

Dr. Simmons glanced back at her file. The next paper was a brightly colored flyer with an image of a smiling infant. She shuffled through a few more similar pages. "I don't see your medical history, Ms. Ross."

"I was treated in Los Angeles. I've only just cleared the two-year mark since I ended breast cancer treatments." Hot tears leaked out of her eyes. "I'm sure the test is a false positive. I can't possibly be…"

She couldn't even dare to hope for a healthy pregnancy after everything she'd been through. How could her depleted body possibly nurture a tiny life?

Beside her, Cody laid the paper on the doctor's desk, his other hand still stroking Jillian's back. "Is there any risk to the child from those treatments? After two years?"

"That isn't my area of expertise." The doctor was writing a note on a new sheet of paper. "I'm giving you a referral to an obstetrician who specializes in pregnancy and cancer survivors." She passed it to Jillian. "But I can tell you that chemotherapy drugs leave the body within days or weeks. I'm not worried about the health of the baby. But you'll want to speak to your oncologist about any risks of recurrence in your disease, Ms. Ross."

Cody squeezed her shoulder protectively.

Jillian nodded, drinking in the reassurance that her pregnancy could be healthy despite the treatments. She stared into the doctor's eyes, certain the woman was being forthright.

"I remember reading that doctors recommend waiting two years before trying to become pregnant." How many times had she read all the brochures in her oncologist's office while waiting to see him? "But I thought that didn't apply to me, because I was under the impression I would lose my fertility."

Cody's fingers stilled on her arm. "Is the risk of miscarriage higher?"

The question punctured the small bubble of hope growing inside her, deflating it.

"That's a question for my colleague, Mr. McNeill." Dr. Simmons turned kindly eyes back to Jillian. "But a great deal depends on your medical history. If you sign release forms at the front desk, I'll request your chart, so we can start monitoring the progress of this pregnancy and do everything we can to make sure mother and baby are both healthy."

A baby.

Only then did the idea sink in as a real possibility. She was pregnant. Jillian had never expected her body to return to normal after her treatments, and she thought she'd been prepared to give her fertilized eggs to someone else to carry, down the road in a distant future. But now, just two years after her treatments had ended, a tiny life grew inside her.

Her child. And Cody's.

Only now, while the doctor discussed the more ordinary concerns about pregnancy, did Jillian let herself consider how different her life was going to be if she successfully carried this man's baby to term.

His hand was still splayed along her upper back, filling the space between her shoulder blades. Warm. Reassuring.

Yet with one look at the set of his jaw, the hollow stare of his blue eyes as he studied the literature before him, Jillian could tell that Cody was reeling from the news. He'd been ready to cut ties with her today. Say goodbye forever.

In an instant, their worlds had changed immeasurably. Because no matter how much this independent Wyoming cowboy wanted to remain unfettered and free, Cody's life was now bound to hers through this child they shared.

Nine

A baby.

Cody listened carefully to the doctor's answers to all his questions, knowing he'd think of more once they left. He needed all the information he could get to do everything in his power to make sure Jillian remained healthy.

She looked even more shell-shocked than he felt at the baby news, so he knew that how he handled things going forward was important. He didn't want to upset her. And he needed to stay close to her. As they left Dr. Simmons's office that afternoon, he treaded carefully. Her appointment with the obstetrician specializing in cancer patients in Denver wasn't until tomorrow afternoon, but he wanted to see if they could consult with any other local doctors who might tell them more.

He didn't want to overwhelm her, though.

"Are you all right?" He studied her face in the sunlight, searching for clues to how she was feeling.

Worried? Full of regret? Ready to run? He truly had no idea how she was handling this.

"I'm just so stunned." She hesitated beside the car he recognized as hers, then rested a hand on the fender and closed her eyes for a long moment.

"Would you let me drive you home? Or to my office behind Wrangler's? We could head over there, maybe get something to eat from the bar and bring it in back with us where it's quiet." He liked the plan. They wouldn't see any of his family there. And he didn't think either of them was ready to face outsiders. "I'd like to make a few phone calls to see if we can learn more today. My father is friends with the chief of staff at Cheyenne Regional. I could give him a call and see if there's anyone in oncology who could answer questions for us."

"Sure." She nodded, her eyes unfocused when she opened them. "I would appreciate that. I'd like to call my doctor back home, too. See if I can speak to anyone in the office there."

"Of course." Cody took the papers she held and added them to his stack, then slid a hand around her elbow. "The truck's over here."

She followed him through the parking lot to his pickup. He unlocked the passenger door for her.

"I know we have a lot to talk about," she said, pausing and meeting his gaze directly before stepping into the vehicle. "But I wonder if we could table the discussion until we find out more?"

"I understand." He nodded, recognizing the fear in her voice. "We'll find out all we can and then figure this out."

A baby required their absolute focus and attention, yes. But he understood that Jillian's health could be at risk. And he didn't feel equipped to address her concerns until he knew more about what she'd been through. More about what she might face in the next nine months.

No wonder she was afraid.

As he fired up the truck engine to drive them to his office, he felt his grip on the steering wheel slip a bit. He'd never had sweaty palms in the rodeo arena when he could have been trampled to death on any given night. But right now, thinking about something happening to Jillian or this baby she carried, he was scared as hell.

Scarlett could get used to this life.

She tipped her head back against the seat in the limo. It was shortly after sunset, and the Hollywood lights were already bright. Neon red and blue splashed the bare skin of her calves, filtering through the tinted windows as they slowed for a stop sign. She'd been in Los Angeles for five days, shopping and getting her bearings, sending out a few feelers to friends she'd met at parties over the years.

Confronting Logan King wouldn't be easy when she hadn't seen him in months. She needed trusted intel to figure out where he was going to be and—hopefully—not make it seem like she was seeking him out on purpose. It would undermine her goals if word got back to Logan that she was looking for him. Better for her confrontation to be a surprise.

Though if he happened to hear she was in town, conquering Hollywood and being seen with the hottest celebs of the moment, that was just fine.

The sooner he started eating his heart out, the better. Besides, what kind of actress would she be if she couldn't convince Logan King that he meant nothing to her? Tonight wasn't just about her and Logan, anyway. She was dedicating this performance to every woman who'd ever had a man ignore her. Every woman who'd felt the snub when "I'll call you" actually meant "it's over."

When the limo rolled to a stop in front of Lucerno, the West Hollywood club where Logan was rumored to be this evening for an unofficial wrap party with a handful of other actors, it quickly became the object of side-eye glances from the dozens of people waiting in line for admittance. The vehicle vibrated slightly from the music pouring out the open doors behind the burly bouncer checking a guest list. Pink light glowed from inside the club, the occasional strobe flashing.

Ignoring an attack of nerves, Scarlett squeezed her tiny leather clutch, refusing to give in to an urge to check her makeup. She looked as good as she ever would. She'd painstakingly applied her gold eyeshadow, expertly glued her false eyelashes. She couldn't help the prominent nose, the chin that wasn't quite as strong as she would have liked. That was what highlighting palettes were for.

When the driver opened her door, Scarlett handled the fear the same way she'd handled bronc riding during those years when her father had guilted her into competing to "toughen her up." She charged straight through the heart of it, as fast as possible.

"Scarlett McNeill," she informed the bouncer, not bothering to stand in line.

Chin up. Look like you belong.

She must have fooled a few people, because some of the club-goers waiting in line had pulled out their phones to record her arrival. She hoped her movie studio contact had added her name to that list. The woman was an assistant to a casting director, a friend from a summer theater program Scarlett had joined during her semester abroad in London. While just an elective for her agri-business degree, the theater work had been the most fun she'd had during her university years. With any luck, Lucie was already inside wait-ing for her.

"Have a good time," the bouncer told her, mov-ing aside the velvet rope to admit her, not even bothering to check his list.

"Thank you." She gave him a smile and strode down the steps into the sprawling club, where the pink glow got more intense. Would that small victory be an indication of how the rest of the night went? Or would it be her last win?

Heading for the bar across the dance floor, she spotted her friend Lucie, one of the few people in her life besides her sisters who knew what Logan had done to her.

Reed-thin and almost six feet tall, Lucie was easy to spot in a crowd. She could pull anything off a vintage clothing rack and make it look amazing. Tonight she was wearing a sheer floral dress over a tiny jean skirt.

"Darling, you were born to rock those boots," Lucie announced, hugging Scarlett briefly before holding her at arm's length to admire her. "When are you going to leave farm life behind and move here? I can't survive another Hollywood lunch full of fake smiles and air kisses unless I know I can dish about it with you."

She and Lucie had talked about getting an apartment together in LA. While Scarlett could afford her own place with the monthly income from her share of the ranch earnings, she wanted the bohemian experience that she hadn't gotten in college, and to hear industry gossip on a daily basis.

"If *Winning the West* is filmed in my backyard—and it sounds like it will be—I'm going to stay long enough to watch." Her sister had texted her just last night that Carson signed the agreement with the production company. "But after that wraps, there's nothing keeping me in Cheyenne."

Lucie squeezed her arm. "That's what I want to hear. And speaking of *Winning the West*, the future star of that picture is seated at a private table in the Red Room." She pointed to the far wall with a drink in hand, silver bangles sliding down her arm. "Just past that curtain."

Scarlett's heart beat quicker as she anticipated the confrontation. She dreaded it a little, but knew she had to go through with this. A man jostled her from behind, and she turned to see him dart away, a blur of pinstripe jacket and jeans in the strobe lights.

"Then I know where I'm headed." Scarlett's hand went to her hairdo before she could remind herself she wasn't allowed to be self-conscious.

"You're flawless," Lucie insisted, reading her mind the way only a good friend could. "Go tell him what you think of his games." She held out her half-finished beverage. "Bonus points if you toss my drink in his face."

"No need. I've been working on my script." Scarlett had been writing and rewriting her dialogue in her mind for days. Weeks, really, since she'd been dreaming of her revenge speech even before she'd decided to come to Hollywood and face him.

She charged in the direction of the Red Room, a raised nook off the dance floor draped with red curtains to conceal its VIP occupants. Scarlett wasn't going to give this man the satisfaction of seeing her angry. Of thinking he mattered that much.

She expected to see him at a table full of beautiful, young celebutantes, surrounded by expensive champagne bottles and hangers-on. Instead, her first glimpse of Logan King when she entered the room showed him in deep conversation with another man, someone older and dressed more like a banker or a lawyer, his hand on a briefcase under the round table.

Logan was even more attractive than she remembered. Chiseled jaw. Great hair. Wide green eyes with long lashes and heavy, dark eyebrows. Lips made for kissing. He wore a black jacket over a plain gray T-shirt, his excellent physique under wraps. Still, his jacket stretched a bit around his biceps where he bent his arms to rest on the table. Women danced nearby, as if hoping to be noticed by the newly A-list actor with a bottle of seltzer in front of him.

Caught off guard a bit, Scarlett hesitated. She had gone through numerous scenarios in her head. None of them had played out quite like this. She glanced back to the dance floor, wondering if she should make another pass by the table later. But then she heard her name in that familiar voice.

"Scarlett?"

Even now, her brain bursting with her "screw you" speech, hearing her name on his lips did something funny to her insides. *Damn him.*

Forcing herself to slide into character—a strong woman with a killer sense of self—she squared her shoulders to face him.

"Have we met?" she asked, her heart pounding a mile a minute as she pretended not to know him. That was phase one of her put-down—letting him think he was entirely forgettable, too.

He excused himself from the table and rose to his feet, his eyes on her the whole time.

A waitress passed her with a tray of drinks, and Scarlett stepped sideways to give the woman room. She almost ran into a man—the same guy from the bar wearing the pin-striped jacket with jeans. What was his issue? Had he been following her around the club?

Flustered to be distracted when she had an important job to do, Jillian returned her attention to Logan, who was suddenly standing very close to her. Nearby, the DJ put on a new record, driving more people to the dance floor as the energy kicked into high gear around them. The banker guy Logan had been talking to was gone. A few of the dancing girls slithered back down to the main floor with their sexy moves.

And Logan never took his eyes off her.

"You dropped this." He retrieved a folded sheet

of paper from the floor beside her left foot. When he passed it to her, his arm brushed hers. "And I don't blame you for not wanting to remember me. But I sure haven't forgotten you."

Scarlett knew then she would never make it as an actress. All her memorized lines faded from her brain. Words failed her, period. She stared at him like a gaping fish, her jaw hanging open until she at last thought to close it.

"That's not mine," she said finally, glancing down at the folded stationery.

"That guy just handed it to you," Logan insisted, taking her hand and tucking the note into her palm. "And for what it's worth, I'm glad to see you again."

Jamming the paper in her clutch purse, Scarlett got the jolt she needed when she heard those words.

"You're glad to see me?" She could not believe the gall of some men. Especially too-handsome-for-their-own-good actors. "No wonder you're the toast of Hollywood casting directors. That's one hell of an acting job."

She hadn't wanted to show him anger. In her mind, she'd imagined giving him more of a cool, ice princess speech. But apparently, she didn't have enough ice in her veins.

"Scarlett, about that—"

"No." She cut him off, unwilling to listen to lame excuses. She'd flown across four states to tell him exactly what she thought of him. "You made your decision about me long ago. Did it hurt me at the time? Sure it did. But getting some distance from you has helped me see you weren't worth keeping in my life, anyhow. Turns out that sometimes not getting what you want is a wonderful stroke of luck."

She'd cobbled that together from fragments of other speeches she'd memorized. And it felt good to tell him what she thought. Logan shook his head, his brows scrunched as if he couldn't possibly understand that she was telling him off.

"Furthermore," she continued, warming to the task, "the first step to getting what you want in life is getting rid of what you don't want." She smiled tightly. "I know now that you're what I don't want. Goodbye, Logan. And in the future, have the common courtesy of telling a woman that you're not interested in a relationship, instead of just ignoring her texts when you jet off to film your next movie. That's what grown men do."

Turning on her heel, she walked away from him. It wasn't the powerful performance she'd visualized in her daydreams, but it wasn't half bad.

Or so she thought. Right up until Logan called to her.

"That movie I was filming? It was shot on location in the Republic of the Congo."

She wasn't sure what that had to do with her, so Scarlett kept right on walking.

Before she made it back to Lucie, Logan caught up to her, his breath warm in her ear as he said, "One of the worst places on earth for connectivity."

She paused beside a screen broadcasting images of the dancing crowd, the lights and colors swirling and reflecting off her gold dress.

"That may be the worst excuse ever."

"True. But ask yourself, if I was happy about the split, why would I bother to make an excuse?"

Scarlett knew better than to fall for that. Didn't she? In that moment of hesitation, a camera flashed nearby, the streak of light just another headache-inducing strobe across her vision.

Logan took her elbow and swiveled her away from the camera while she struggled to process what was happening.

"Now, like it or not, we're going to be connected in the tabloids." He ushered her toward a back door marked Exit behind the huge screen, skillfully edging his way around people grinding in the shadows of the dance floor. "You can yell at me all you want outside, but I'm unwilling to make a bigger scene than we already have."

Driving back toward the White Canyon Ranch after their evening consultation with the oncologist, Cody knew they couldn't put it off any longer. He'd done his best to honor Jillian's wishes to table the discussion about the baby. But they'd spent the day learning more about her cancer and more about the possible obstacles they faced in this pregnancy. His father's friend at Cheyenne Regional Medical Center had gotten them a meeting with an on-call oncologist, a busy man who'd given them half an hour of his time to talk about their concerns and to review Jillian's medical history.

They would learn more tomorrow when they met with the specialist. But Cody wanted to talk about it tonight, if only to reassure Jillian. To let her know he supported her in whatever happened.

"Would you consider spending the night at the Black Creek?" he asked, as the truck bounced over a pothole. "I can make us something to eat, and we'll have more privacy to talk than at the guest ranch."

"Okay." Her voice was small. Far-off. She sounded different from the determined woman he'd come to know. He glanced across the truck cab to see her staring into the distance out the passenger-side window.

"There's plenty of space. You can have your

own room, of course." He didn't mean to make assumptions about their relationship.

"Thank you." She said no more.

He couldn't tell if she was frightened about what a pregnancy could mean for her health, or if she was thinking about what it meant for the two of them as a couple. But she had to be reeling.

"We should talk about this, Jillian." He knew they needed to start thinking about what came next. "I know we agreed to wait until we learned more, but after tonight's meeting—"

"We've known each other for just over a week." She shifted on the leather seat, turning toward him as he steered the truck down a back road. "And I realize this is far more than you ever bargained for when you asked me to dance that night."

The road here was lit only by stars and the two beams of his headlights, but it wasn't nearly as tough to navigate as this conversation.

"I remember asking for a whole lot more than a dance." He had no intention of bowing out of this situation, if that's what she was thinking. "We both did. And we both knew the consequences."

"Honestly, I didn't." She shook her head slowly. In disbelief. "I thought I would be sterile. For years, and maybe forever." She hugged her arms around herself, sitting back in the seat. "You're the only person I've been with since my treatment, because I was having trouble feeling at all desirable."

He reached across the console to rest his hand on her knee, to offer whatever comfort he could. He wanted to wrap her up tight in his arms and keep her safe for the next nine months. Hell, longer than that. Their lives were inextricably entwined now. As the mother of his child, Jillian would come under his protection forever. He'd accepted that fact the moment he'd seen the test results, but he didn't want to overwhelm her with any more than what she was already dealing with today.

"I can't pretend to know what you're going through right now. It's a lot even for me to process, and I know there's far more at stake for you." He couldn't stand the idea of this pregnancy hurting her. What if it triggered her cancer?

The oncologist had insisted there was no definitive proof the hormones from pregnancy could spur a recurrence. He'd cited the most current studies, which showed no difference in recurrence rates between women who got pregnant after breast cancer treatment and women who didn't.

But those studies were very new. And apparently Jillian had only recently stopped her course of hormone blockers. Cody had learned a lot about cancer today, and while he'd found it all scary as hell, he also had renewed appreciation for what she'd gone through in her treatments.

"I've been through every emotion today," she admitted, as he drove the truck under the welcome sign for the ranch. "Happiness and fear, worry and awe. And maybe I should feel guilty for misleading you, but I really thought—"

"You have nothing to feel guilty about." He parked next to the front door, not bothering to put the truck in the garage when he wanted to get her inside and feed her.

"But I assured you there was no chance I could get pregnant. I guess if I'd known it was a possibility, I could have taken contraception after the fact, but I was so certain—"

"You didn't know. You told me the same things your doctors told you. I understand that." He switched off the truck and pocketed the keys. He went around to her side of the pickup to help her down, then led her to the front door of the main house.

She'd been on the property before, but not inside the house. He would never have dreamed these would be the circumstances for her introduction to the place—newly pregnant with his child. The news still staggered him.

He showed her into his home, flipping on light switches as they headed through the living area toward the kitchen.

"Have a seat and I'll make us something to eat. You must be exhausted." He slid a leather-padded stool from the breakfast bar for her, then started pulling ingredients out of the refrigerator. He could have messaged his housekeeper to prepare dinner for them, but he had a strong desire to cook for Jillian himself. To keep his hands busy as an outlet for the fear running through him.

For her. For their child.

Jillian opened the sheaf of papers they'd collected throughout the day—pamphlets from the obstetrician's office and the oncologist. She scanned the contents of one of the sheets while he turned on the gas flame under a cast-iron skillet. Her finger followed the lines of text on the page.

"You realize one of the risks of finding out about a pregnancy this early is that if I miscarry in the first few weeks, we'll both know it was a miscarriage." She glanced up from the paperwork. "Whereas if we'd waited for a missed period, we would have never known about it."

"I thought of that." He hated the knowledge that he might have brought her more pain by insisting on a blood test so soon. He chopped tomatoes and peppers. "And I'm sorry if it turns out I could have spared you that hurt."

"I'm going to think positively," she insisted. "Last week I thought there was zero chance of getting pregnant, so I've already had good news on that score. Although it does say here that even healthy women have a 10 to 25 percent chance of miscarrying in the early weeks."

He swallowed back the fresh wave of worry for her. How devastated would she be to lose a child after all she'd already been through? He chopped faster, adding mushrooms to the mix as the vegetables started to sizzle in the pan.

"If there's anything at all I can do or offer you to help make sure you stay healthy, I will. Whatever you want or need, it's yours." He cracked eggs on top of the half-cooked veggies. His temples throbbed with thoughts about all the ways this pregnancy could go wrong. Then, after wiping his hands on a kitchen towel, he came around to stand beside her at the breakfast bar and took her hands in his. "But Jillian, if you are worried about the cancer coming back, or if we find out from the specialist that this pregnancy increases your risk of recurrence, I would understand if—"

"No." Shaking her head, she squeezed his hands hard. "This pregnancy is nothing short of a miracle to me. I never expected it, and the timing isn't what I imagined, but after all the nights I've shed tears thinking I might not ever have children, I'll do everything in my power to make sure this is a healthy pregnancy."

Some of the tension inside him eased. But the fear for her still twisted like a knot in his chest. He had watched, helpless, as his mother died. He couldn't let anything happen to Jillian. He would do whatever it took to keep her safe.

"I understand." He wrapped his arms around her, hugging her gently before straightening. "And I want to help in any way I can. For starters, I'd like you to move in with me."

Ten

Jillian let the idea settle in her brain, knowing it was too soon to think long-term, but feeling tempted anyhow. Or maybe it was just the draw of Cody's arms around her that had her considering his proposition for one crazy moment. How often during her treatments had she craved the kind of emotional support he knew how to give?

Cody McNeill would never abandon a woman after surgery to remove a tumor the way her ex-boyfriend had. Honor and responsibility were coded in his very DNA, were a rock-solid part of his character. But Jillian knew that he would offer that support to any woman who carried his child. His suggestion that they live together didn't have anything to do with her. It had everything to do with his baby.

"That's a big step," she told him carefully, not wanting to appear ungrateful. She edged back from his embrace, needing to look into his eyes.

"So is a baby."

She couldn't argue with that. It touched her heart that he would sacrifice his own happiness to provide for her and their child. And at the same time, it hurt to know she'd never be able to differentiate his feelings for her from his sense of duty.

"I just feel like it's too soon. Especially when we agreed to table any discussion until we learned more about my health. More about—" she couldn't bring herself to think about the chance of losing the pregnancy; not when the idea of being a mother was starting to take hold as a possibility for her "—the baby."

She mourned the loss of Cody's touch already. Wished she could have lingered in the circle of his arms, if only to pretend everything was going to be all right. He slid the pan off the stove and turned the burner off.

"Then we'll wait." He nodded brusquely. "We'll see what tomorrow brings and revisit the idea after we speak to the specialist. For now, we can have some dinner, and then I'll let you rest. You deserve a good night's sleep after the day you've had."

They both did. She knew this wasn't easy for him, either. That his life would have been so much simpler if she hadn't gotten pregnant.

"Thank you." She needed to retreat. To try to process this news. To figure out what would be best for her future and her child's.

"After I serve us, I'll show you to your room and make sure you have everything you need," he said, sliding the food onto their plates and setting them on the kitchen counter. He was the perfect host. Attentive. Thoughtful.

She should be thankful he took this news seriously. And she was. But a part of her couldn't help missing the man she'd danced with at Wrangler's that first night. The Cody McNeill who'd been ready to abandon caution, and share life's next adventure with her.

The next afternoon, after her exam, Jillian got dressed and then followed the nurse into Dr. Webster's spacious corner office. Cody was already there; he'd driven her to the appointment, stopped by the White Canyon Ranch to pick up her things and then returned so they could meet with the doctor together. When she entered the room, he waited for her to take a seat in front of the mahogany desk then sat next to her. They didn't have time to speak privately, however, before the doctor arrived.

Cody stood and the two men shook hands. When Cody settled into the chair beside her again, he slid his hand around hers and squeezed. She wondered if he did that without thinking, to seek contact with her, or if it was a conscious attempt to offer her comfort.

Not that it necessarily mattered. It was a kindness either way, and there was no denying his actions touched her. Yet she couldn't help but wonder whether, if she moved in with him, she would ever know what gestures were real and which were a product of his strong sense of responsibility. He already viewed himself as the responsible one in his family—the one who managed the core of the McNeill ranching business while his siblings pursued outside interests like acting or the rodeo.

If a good night's sleep had made Jillian realize only one thing about this pregnancy, it was that she didn't want to be another person on his list of responsibilities, no matter how seductive his touch was.

"Do you have questions for me?" Dr. Webster was asking, reminding Jillian that she needed to focus on the here and now. She'd missed half of his remarks about her health, but then, the obstetrician had given her his views about her pregnancy prospects when they'd been in the exam room. Up until now, he'd simply been bringing Cody up to speed.

In the obstetrician's opinion, she had as much chance as any woman of carrying a baby to full term. Breastfeeding most likely wouldn't be an option, but he didn't rule that out, either. His patients' experiences with pregnancy and cancer reflected the findings of the recent European study the doctors had mentioned to Jillian and Cody yesterday—that pregnancy hormones did not spur a recurrence of breast cancer.

"You've reviewed Jillian's chart from her medical team in Los Angeles," Cody began, glancing her way a moment before he encircled her shoulders with one arm. "In your opinion, regardless of pregnancy, what is the risk of her disease returning?"

She understood why he needed to ask the question. If she succumbed to a second round of cancer, he would be the sole parent to this child. Cody deserved to know the answer so he could be ready. Still, all the rationalizing in the world didn't lessen the pain that came with those words. The reminder of the shadow cancer cast over her whole life, even now.

It meant the possibility that she would miss out

on seeing her child grow up. The stakes were higher than ever. She needed to remain healthy.

"Her risk of contracting breast cancer a second time is slightly higher than the average woman's, but not significantly so. It helps tremendously that her disease isn't hereditary. With no family history working against her, she has every reason to feel more optimistic." The doctor's words echoed those of other medical professionals she'd dealt with during her treatments.

She was lucky that her cancer wasn't hereditary, they'd all agreed two years ago. It had been difficult to feel fortunate, however, when she'd been so ill she'd thought she wouldn't survive the vile drugs they'd given her. When the burns from radiation had reduced her to tears, her skin hurting so badly she couldn't sleep without more powerful drugs. Often, she'd refused the pain medicine, not wanting to introduce even more chemicals to a body overflowing with them.

Cody stroked her arm. Her back. His touch felt familiar. Comforting. She wanted to lean into him, but she couldn't afford to lose her independence now. Not when she had a baby's future to consider.

She regretted that her health concerns gave him far more to grapple with than if she'd been whole. Cancer-free. Yet she couldn't change who she was or what had happened between them. She could only move forward. One foot ahead of the other.

"Where do we go from here?" she asked, focusing on the future. "How often should I be checked?"

The doctor confirmed what she'd read in the literature the night before—that she had to bear in mind that a percentage of all pregnancies ended in miscarriage without the mother even realizing she'd been pregnant. He set up a schedule to monitor her hormone levels over the upcoming weeks, which meant more blood tests. He also gave them more literature on healthy diet and exercise, stressing the importance of minimizing all other risk factors.

Cody listened carefully, asking more questions, his face carved with lines of worry. His strong shoulders were set in a rigid posture, as if he had to bear all this alone. She understood his fear. She shared it, of course. Yet Jillian was familiar with all the doctor's suggestions. She'd already heard these lectures and read the brochures. She was already doing everything she could to stay healthy. Aside from that glass of wine she'd ordered in the Thirsty Cow the night she met Cody, she'd been a model of good behavior.

But she couldn't stop living because of the disease, or else cancer won. Yes, she would take extra precautions while she was pregnant, since she really did consider it a miracle that she'd conceived at all. Once she'd given birth, though, if she was lucky enough to carry this baby to term, she refused to live in a padded box. She needed to *live*, and that meant continuing to enjoy her list of life adventures. The only way to defy the disease was not just to exist, but to thrive.

As Cody asked the doctor for additional literature on food guidelines and risk factors, Jillian wondered if the responsible father of her child would understand that.

When they emerged from the physician's office half an hour later, a schedule for follow-up visits in hand, Jillian debated how to broach the topic with him. They had known each other so briefly, it was almost impossible to gauge how he might react. But they needed to have some difficult conversations, and soon. From the last time they'd slept together—when the earth had moved for her, but Cody had tried to distance himself from her afterward by asking about the blood test—Jillian knew that he didn't want to date and wasn't interested in furthering a relationship.

So she couldn't afford to let her emotions make the decisions for her.

"We should talk," she told him as he opened the door of his truck for her. She had a lot of things to weigh, and she knew he did, too.

When he didn't answer right away, she peered over at him and saw he'd taken out his phone. She'd noticed last night that it had chimed often, but he'd never checked it once when they'd been discussing the pregnancy. Now, remembering that, along with his concerns about his father and sister, she hesitated before taking her seat.

"Is everything okay with your family?"

He looked up, frowning. "I'm sorry. I was getting so many messages in there, I was worried something serious had happened."

"What is it?"

"See for yourself." He flipped his phone around so she could view a photo of Scarlett and a familiar-looking man filling the screen.

She read the caption aloud, "'Scarlett McNeill, heiress to a cattle ranch fortune, seems to have caught the eye of sought-after playboy Logan King, according to partygoers at a West Hollywood hotspot last night.'" Jillian's gaze flew to Cody's. "This is the actor slated to star in *Winning the West*."

That's why she knew the young man's face—from the director's notes. Logan was handsome enough in a traditional sense—he had, quite literally, movie-star good looks. She couldn't help but compare his style to Cody's more rugged appeal, though. She certainly knew which man she'd choose every time. She guessed Logan King was the actor Scarlett had met. Possibly the same man Paige didn't want her daughter to see.

"Right. So now Carson will get to host a Hollywood playboy looking for an heiress to fund his expensive tastes." Cody jammed the phone into his pocket. "My father will be thrilled," he said drily.

"I'm sure the story is overblown." Jillian hadn't been in the industry long, but she'd seen enough false tabloid reports to know they had no shame when it came to manipulating stories to make a good headline. "Logan King's star is on the rise, and so is the price he commands per film. I doubt he's romancing Scarlett because of her fortune."

Cody shook his head. Only now did Jillian notice the dark circles under his eyes. No doubt he hadn't slept much the night before, between worry about her and worry about his family.

"Damned if I know. But apparently the interest in our family has skyrocketed." He took her hand and eased her into the pickup. "Maddy's been taking reservations for the White Canyon all day, and her website crashed from too much traffic. Brock had to kick out a reporter who was nosing around the barns this morning, so I'm going to look into increasing security before the film crew rolls into town."

Too stunned to argue, Jillian buckled her seat belt while he slid into the driver's side. "I never would have guessed the movie would bring that kind of attention."

"This surge of interest is because of Scarlett, not *Winning the West*." Cody steered the pickup toward the outskirts of town and the Black Creek Ranch, a route she was beginning to know well.

A route that quickly turned rural, and then downright picturesque. The highway leading northwest offered breathtaking views of the Laramie Mountains, with the sky so blue behind them they stood in stark three-dimensional relief. Even the air was different than Southern California, where the ocean breezes could turn heavy with smog. Here, the almost constant wind felt crisp and clean, every day a fresh start.

"Has anyone in your family spoken to Scarlett? What's her take on this?"

"Maisie texted with her briefly this morning, but only enough for Scarlett to say that we're supposed to 'ignore the rumors.' Whatever that means." Cody drummed his thumbs lightly on the steering wheel. "Although to be truthful, I haven't read through all those group messages on my phone. As you know, I have more important things on my mind."

Jillian felt that pull of attraction to him again, less physical this time, and more emotional. She appreciated how he'd handled things so far, even though she recognized they hadn't begun to truly figure out what this baby would mean for them. Yet Cody took the potential complications seriously. And he hadn't pushed her to talk when she wasn't ready.

But would the man who'd asked her to move in with him be able to let her go when the time came?

"I do welcome the break from thinking about our situation, though." She cracked the truck window to let some of that warm summer air flow through her hair and blow away some of the fears. "I went to bed scared last night, and I woke up scared today. So I'm grateful to think about your sister for a few minutes instead."

"Then, if you don't mind—" Cody retrieved his phone from his pocket and passed it to her, keeping his eyes on the road "—would you mind glancing through the group messages? See if there's anything urgent in there?"

"Are you sure?" She studied his face, but didn't turn on the device. Funny to think she'd slept with him twice yet hesitated to touch his phone.

"There's nothing in there you can't see." His jaw flexed, the slightest hint of emotion crossing his face, an emotion she couldn't read.

"Okay." She switched on the phone. "No password?" She opened his messages easily, seeing the slew of new ones on the same group thread.

"I'm an open book." There was definitely a hint of something defiant in his voice.

"Call me crazy, but I sense a story there." She scanned the messages for him while he turned off the interstate onto the private road that led to the ranch.

"I found out my last girlfriend was cheating when her phone buzzed about fifty times while she was in the shower. I grabbed it to bring to her, thinking the constant messages could be important. But the screen filled with private texts from another guy."

Jillian's finger stilled on the glass surface of the screen. "I'm so sorry."

"Don't be. It's always better to know." His scowl said otherwise, but she wasn't going to argue. "She defended her faithlessness by saying I was too cold to love."

Ouch. The woman must have been blind if she couldn't see the way Cody showed his love for his family by taking on the role of protector and provider. Already Jillian had been swept up into that world now that she was pregnant with his child, landing on the list of people he wouldn't let down.

"Some people go into attack mode when they feel cornered." She flicked the screen on again to finish scrolling. "She probably would have said anything to deflect attention from her own short-comings."

"What about you?" he asked, glancing Jillian's way. The muscle in his jaw twitched as he frowned. "I hope no one you ever cared about went into attack mode."

She closed her eyes for a moment, remembering old hurts and finding they were nothing compared to all she'd been through since then.

"My ex-boyfriend bailed on me right after my first surgery." She could see now what a pale shadow of a man he'd been, especially in comparison to Cody. Ethan had been interesting enough when their lives were easy, but a crisis had revealed his character. "He said the surgery had been hard enough. He couldn't handle chemo and radiation, too."

"*He* couldn't handle it?" The outrage in Cody's voice was strangely comforting.

"That's a direct quote."

"Good riddance." His grip tightened on the

steering wheel, knuckles flexing. "Although I'm sure it didn't seem like it at the time."

"I realized I hadn't really loved him when my main worry after the breakup was how to get to my appointments when I was sick and tired." She'd been so exhausted, and hadn't liked relying on her aging parents, who lived in a small town in Northern California. "But I met a lot of truly lovely Uber drivers during that time in my life."

Cody swore softly and rested a broad, steady hand on her knee for a quick squeeze. "You're never going to have to drive yourself to another appointment again."

The certainty in that promise rattled her, especially when she needed to tell him that Cheyenne couldn't be her forever home. But she wasn't ready yet. Not now. For all they knew, this pregnancy wouldn't last out the month. She would be devastated if she miscarried, but considering the hell her body had been through, she wouldn't be surprised.

As he pulled into the driveway in front of the main house, she was just as glad to sidestep that topic a little longer. Instead, she focused on the text messages from his family.

One that seemed important caught her eye as he slid out of the driver's seat and came around to her side.

"Cody?" She flipped the phone for him to see, hoping she was misunderstanding what she was reading. "It looks like your father is worried that your stepmother has gone missing."

"Impossible." His blue eyes narrowed as he took the device, helping her down with his free hand. "Paige hardly ever leaves the ranch, let alone Cheyenne."

"Maybe she went to see Scarlett?" Jillian remembered the exchange she'd witnessed between mother and daughter the night of the rodeo. Something had seemed off.

"But why?" Cody thumbed through more messages. "Scarlett has enjoyed being the center of attention since she was old enough to talk. Why would her mother worry about her dating some Hollywood dude? It's inconvenient for us, maybe, but I picture Scarlett being thrilled right now."

Jillian didn't have any answers.

"Paige will turn up." He turned off the phone again and slid his arm around her waist. "We've got more pressing matters to think about now. Let me make you dinner and we can figure out what to do if this baby is as stubborn a fighter as his mom."

"His?" She shouldn't allow herself to be charmed by Cody, but felt her heart soften a little anyhow.

"Or hers." He planted a tender kiss on her temple. "If she's as tough as her mom, we're going to need to make some plans for life nine months from now."

Jillian closed her eyes for a moment as they stood there on the front porch. She let herself imagine what it would be like to parent a baby with this honorable, responsible, thoughtful man. To stay in this awe-inspiring part of the country that had captured her imagination so thoroughly she was bringing a whole movie to town to share the beauty of it with the world.

But if ever she needed to be strong, it was right

now. Because if this pregnancy lasted and they shared a child, Jillian wouldn't accept a supporting role while Cody McNeill called the shots. No matter how charming he could be, she knew that keeping his child close was going to be his number one priority. She didn't have any intention of giving up all her dreams to be stuck in a loveless relationship.

Cody might not be cold, the way his ex-girlfriend had accused him of being. But he certainly didn't love Jillian. Which meant this conversation he wanted to have was not going to end well.

"Cody, I'm worried about your family." It was the truth, she realized, as the words fell out of her mouth. Yes, she wanted to delay this conversation with him about the future. But she couldn't imagine this strong Wyoming family of his messaging each other twenty times in a day unless something serious was happening. She didn't want the pregnancy news to distract him from something important developing with the rest of the McNeills.

"I don't think we need to worry about Scarlett." His expression was resolute. "Besides, I'm not going to be the one who stops her from living her dreams." He leveled a knowing look at Jillian, reminding her of their argument about personal freedom versus family duty.

"But what about your dad? Your stepmom? Shouldn't you make sure they're okay?" She had barely gotten to know his family, hadn't even met his father or his grandfather.

She'd never had a big, extended family the way he did. And if they one day shared a child who'd be a part of that larger group, she'd want to know them all very well. It wasn't too soon to start making those connections.

And his family would be all the more important to their child if she relapsed. The thought made Jillian's throat dry up.

Stroking his palms over her shoulders, Cody stared down into her eyes. "I will do whatever you want me to, because I don't want you to worry, and I don't want you to have any stress. But first, be honest with me. Is this a stall tactic from talking about us?"

* * *

He needed trust between them.

After the way his last relationship had ended, having forthright communication was important to him. And although he'd gotten off on the wrong foot with Jillian when she'd mistaken him for Carson, he'd developed more faith in her character since then. He didn't believe she was the kind of woman who would purposely deceive him.

"Yes and no." Jillian's hazel eyes locked on his. "I'm not ready to move into the ranch for good, but if I promise to stay here for the week, we'll have time to talk about the future. But in the meantime, aren't you a little worried about all the texts going back and forth among your family members today? You don't strike me as the kind of family to spend the afternoon texting each other."

He guessed there was more to it that she wasn't sharing, but maybe that was part of the reason she wanted to delay further discussion. He was new to all of this. And he was trying to navigate it with someone he didn't know well enough.

"We definitely aren't." Cody had worries of his own. If his father was including all the family in his messages—even Carson, with whom he was barely on speaking terms—something was wrong. "If you'll let me get you something to eat first, I'll read all these texts and figure out what's going on. I can ride over to my dad's if it seems necessary."

"I'm perfectly capable of making dinner—"

"Please." He didn't want to argue with her. The only thing he had any control over in this pregnancy was his contribution to Jillian's welfare, and he refused to relinquish that role. "I want to help you stay healthy and get enough rest. Make yourself comfortable and let me feed you, then I promise I'll check in with my family."

At her nod, relief rushed through him. He opened the front door before she changed her mind. His gaze followed her slender figure as she retreated up the stairs to the bedroom where she'd spent the previous night.

His thoughts turned to dinner. The doctor had said maintaining a healthy diet was critical, and Cody intended to make sure she had plenty of variety so she could find foods that would appeal to her. Tomorrow, he'd find a chef who was a certified dietician. Someone more skilled in a kitchen than him. For now, he grabbed some steaks and a couple chicken breasts, then fired up the grill.

Jillian would have every possible advantage to help her through this pregnancy. He would see to it personally. She'd agreed to stay with him for one week. He'd simply find a way to romance her. To get to know her better and make her happy. Above all, to ensure that after their week together was over, she never wanted to leave.

Eleven

When Scarlett touched down in Cheyenne at the tiny private airport outside of town, she was surprised to see her grandfather's limousine waiting nearby. The ground crew retrieved her bags while she walked down the steps of the Learjet. Hopefully, she hadn't kept Malcolm McNeill waiting for his plane.

She lifted her hand to wave at the long, dark Mercedes with tinted windows. It had been a quick flight from LA, too quick because she was dreading facing her family when she got home. Her father hated publicity and the limelight in general, but he especially disliked the superficial kind that came from celebrity stalkers and paparazzi—the kind she'd garnered when she'd been in Hollywood. He'd messaged her a terse command to see him upon her return, and she planned to make his house her first stop so she could get the confrontation over with.

Which reminded her of the last showdown she'd had with a man: Logan King. She had held strong against thinking about him—sort of—last night. But when she woke up to the photos of them together plastered all over the internet, she had weakened. She'd stared at them far too long. Before she knew it, she'd found herself searching for articles about the film shoot in the Congo. Two supporting actors had quit during the grueling months shooting in Africa, a time made more difficult by a demanding director who'd closed the set to "bond" his team. After Logan returned to the United States, he'd said in an interview that it had been the most challenging experience of his life.

What if it wasn't just a sound bite? Frustrated

to still be thinking about him, Scarlett focused on her grandfather instead.

Just then, the Mercedes driver got out of the vehicle, hurried around to the back and opened the door to reveal Rose Hanson, Malcolm McNeill's new girlfriend. The woman stepped onto the tarmac, holding a fistful of her long, colorful gauze skirt in one hand to keep it from blowing in the wind. Her long gray hair was in a thick braid draped over one shoulder. She waved at Scarlett while Malcolm emerged from the car behind her, his crisp blue suit making him look every inch the Manhattan business mogul.

"Hello, Granddad. Rose." She hugged them both while the driver pulled their luggage from the trunk. "I hope I didn't keep you waiting. I'm so grateful for the use of the plane."

Malcolm waved aside the thanks. She noticed how his thinning gray hair was perfectly in place despite the breeze. "We timed our arrival so we could see you before we left. I talked to the pilot last night, so I knew your schedule."

"Where are you going?" Scarlett had been

under the impression Malcolm would stay in Cheyenne for as long as it took to make peace with his estranged son, her very stubborn father.

"I'm heading to Silicon Valley for a few days to visit my grandson Damon and his wife, Caroline. They have a son that I've yet to meet."

"And my granddaughter, Brianne, will be there visiting with Malcolm's grandson Gabe," Rose added. "So we both get to see grandchildren."

Scarlett had visited Gabe and Brianne and their adorable boy, Jason, on a trip to Martinique last winter. Brianne was just as warmhearted as her grandmother.

"And one shared great-grandchild," Malcolm reminded her, his blue eyes twinkling with mischief as they exchanged smiles.

Rose patted Scarlett's arm. "And one shared great-grandchild. My Brianne loves Gabe's boy like her own. I'm so glad they're coming to the States more now that Damon is in California. They want the cousins to be close."

"That sounds nice," Scarlett admitted, wishing her family would come together the way the rest of Malcolm's heirs had. "I hope we have get-to-gethers like that one day."

Even among the siblings there were disagreements, with Cody and Carson never seeing eye to eye. Brock coped by keeping them all at arm's length. Since Madeline had started dating Sawyer Calderon, from a rival ranching family, tensions ran even higher.

"Malcolm will win over your dad one of these days." Rose took his hand in hers and squeezed it. The gesture was so sweet that Scarlett found herself envying them.

"I left the keys to the house for you in the car, if anyone wants to use the place while we're gone." He'd rented a massive hobby ranch in Cheyenne for the year, in the hope of reconciling with Scarlett's father. "I'm sending the plane back up here, too, in case you need it. Take the limo back home, honey, and we'll see you next week." Her grandfather nodded to the driver, who moved to take Scarlett's bags from the ground crew workers who had carted them over.

After a quick goodbye, Scarlett retreated into

the back seat of the spacious vehicle. She picked up the envelope with her name on it that contained the keys, and slid it into the back pocket of her purse.

Another piece of paper there caught her eye. She'd forgotten all about the note Logan had handed her at the club the night before. She'd been so distracted, so surprised that he would bother defending himself regarding her unreturned texts six months ago, the mystery note had slipped her mind.

Logan thought the man in the pin-striped jacket had passed it to her. How was that possible? She didn't even know the guy.

Now, as the limousine pulled out of the private airport and onto the deserted the backroads that would lead her home, Scarlett unfolded the heavy parchment.

Inside, there was a brief typed message:

Do you know your mother's true identity? You might be surprised to find out her real name. And to learn her marriage to your father was never legal. I will make trouble for your family if you continue your plan to let *Winning the West* be filmed on McNeill land.

Stunned, Scarlett reread the message two times. It couldn't possibly be true.

It must be a trick to stir up trouble. Possibly a prelude to blackmail. Her stomach, already in knots after the unsuccessful trip to LA and the public standoff with Logan that had turned into a paparazzi photo op, churned with fear.

Was there any chance her mother hadn't gotten married using her real name? That Paige Samara McNeill had a hidden past? Normally, her mom was unflappable, the anchor of their family. The voice of reason when her father flew off the handle about something. She was stable. Grounded.

But she had seemed a bit anxious ever since the location scout came to town. And especially since Scarlett had mentioned her plan to fly to Los Angeles for a few days. She'd assumed it was because her mother didn't want her to follow dreams that would take Scarlett out of Cheyenne. What if there was more to it than that?

One thing was certain: Scarlett couldn't walk

into her father's house and face her mother until she had a plan. Pulling her phone from her purse, she punched in her sister Maisie's number and prayed she would answer.

Maisie would make it all go away with a cynical comment about how gullible Scarlett could be. She'd probably say Scarlett was crazy to put any stock in a note from a stranger.

"Scarlett?" Maisie's voice sounded strained when she answered. "Is that you?"

"Yes." Straightening in her seat, Scarlett got ready to tell her all about the note, but Maisie rushed to fill the pause.

"Honey, get over to Dad's house. Mom is missing."

Too shocked to process much beyond that, Scarlett jammed the note back into her purse while Maisie explained that the whole family was gathering at their father's house right now. That Scarlett needed to be home with them.

The mystery message would have to wait. She needed to be there for her father, who must be going out of his mind. If her mother had a hidden past, what if it did more harm than good to reveal the message to the whole family? What was important was finding her.

Scarlett decided to keep the note to herself a little longer. At least until she could speak to one of her sisters privately and ask what she thought about it. Just until they figured out exactly what was happening.

Alone in her suite at the Black Creek Ranch after dinner, Jillian let her fingers wander over the literature from the obstetrician. Pamphlets about a baby's development. Brochures about maternal health. And yes, special notes for cancer survivors who were expecting a child.

Pulling the throw blanket from the back of the love seat over her lap, Jillian scanned the luxurious bedroom suite, complete with king-size bed near windows that led out onto a balcony overlooking the swimming pool and a courtyard. The sunken sitting area had a gas fireplace, and Cody had carefully placed the TV remote on a table within easy reach for her, along with a pitcher of water, a crystal glass, an ice bucket and her cell phone.

A few feet away, he'd crowded a side table with platters of snacks in case she got hungry while he was gone. As if that was possible after the huge, multicourse meal he'd made in short order downstairs. She couldn't possibly eat a strip steak and a whole chicken breast, but they were both delicious and she'd eaten more than she thought she would. Vegetables in a rainbow of colors had filled the rest of her plate; the meal was about as close to the doctor-recommended guidelines for her diet as possible.

Cody's every action told her how much he wanted this baby. How important it was to him to keep her safe. Healthy. It was important to her, too. But she understood that cancer was indiscriminate. That she could take every precaution, follow every guideline on those doctors' lists and still have a recurrence. That was why she couldn't fall into that trap. She refused to play that game where she sacrificed her dreams to cater to her disease's every whim, only to be beaten by the illness in the end.

Grabbing her cell phone, she punched in the phone number she already should have called.

"Hello?" On the other end, her boss—the woman she answered to directly—sounded flustered. Busy.

In the background, Jillian could hear the wail of an infant. The clatter of dishes and running water.

"Hi, Alyssa, it's Jillian. I hope it's not a bad time."

"Not at all. Just trying to get the kidlets to bed before Todd gets home from tennis." Alyssa must have put the phone on speaker because there was some interference, and the noise on her end got louder. "Guys, what do we say to Miss Jillian?"

Alyssa's two girls shrieked, "Hi, Miss Jillian!" at earsplitting volume. A moment later, the baby greeted her with a happy gurgling sound.

"Go to bed for Mom, munchkins, and I'll bring you a prize home from cowboy country." Jillian had gotten to know Alyssa during her chemo treatments. Her boss's eldest son suffered severe rheumatoid arthritis that required chemo, too.

Jack had been fun company during those dark months, his outlook never down in all the times they'd shared a waiting room or a recovery area afterward.

The two little girls squealed some more until Alyssa took the phone off speaker. She must have chased the kids into their beds because it got quiet again.

"How's Jack?" Jillian asked, while Alyssa worked her mom magic with the baby.

In the background, a soft lullaby began playing before her boss responded.

"He's good. Tired from getting back to school after those weeks we had him out with a flare-up, but you know Jack. He keeps going."

"I'm glad he's back at school. I know how much it means to him to feel normal." Jillian remembered what an inspiration the boy had been. He had his own list of life adventures—most of which were far more interesting than hers. She'd laughed so hard when he told her that he was adding Ride a Lawn Mower to School to his list. Thinking about that made her all the more confident in her own decision to keep moving forward. "I'm sorry I didn't check in yesterday. But I think I've got everything in order here for filming to begin. What's my next assignment?"

She took notes while Alyssa reeled off a handful of locations that needed scouting, letting Jillian weigh in on what possibilities sounded the most promising, allowing her to choose her next destination.

Flagstaff or the Pacific Northwest?

She'd never seen the Grand Canyon, and it was on her list. She didn't need to pull it up to know. So, to honor the spirit of adventure that had helped her to conquer cancer the first time, Jillian accepted the Flagstaff scouting job.

After disconnecting the call, the burn in her throat started, the precursor to tears she knew were coming. She didn't want to upset Cody, but she also couldn't afford to stay here and let herself fall the rest of the way in love with him. That last night they'd spent together had rattled her emotions too much already, stirring deep feelings for a man who had looked to her for only a temporary diversion.

She couldn't be another responsibility on his list. This week, they'd hash out a plan for co-parenting. But after that, she needed to move on. Maintaining her independence was more important than ever. If the only legacy she could give her child was the knowledge that she hadn't let cancer keep her down, that she'd chosen to embrace life every moment, that was something Jillian could be proud of.

Cody stood in his parents' small living room, staring out the front window at his siblings' vehicles. Two had arrived on horseback, their animals tied to the front porch rail as if the house was a saloon in some old Western flick. No wonder Jillian thought a movie ought to be shot here.

Behind Brock's quarter horse and Maisie's spirited Appaloosa, their father's ATV sat beside Maddy's brand-new sports car. On the grass in the side field he could see Carson's pickup truck parked beside his own. They'd both bought the same model year—one gray, one black—within days of each other. Seeing the trucks side by side made Cody shake his head. He might scoff at being anything like his twin, but the similarities came out in those kinds of choices.

Proving you didn't escape family.

He glanced across the living room at his twin now, grateful Carson had put in an appearance when their father had asked for them all to be here. Their dad paced in the kitchen, waiting for Scarlett to arrive. Maisie and Maddy were in their mother's bedroom at Dad's request, looking around to see if they noticed anything missing. Cody was anxious to get the family meeting underway because, while he was concerned about his stepmother's whereabouts, his thoughts were preoccupied by Jillian and her pregnancy. They hadn't even scratched the surface of all they needed to discuss. His brain was working a mile a minute thinking through plans. Moving her to Wyoming. Helping her settle in.

Asking her to marry him. He didn't want to

rush her, but that had to be a consideration. He didn't plan to have his child come into the world without the security that marriage brought to a family.

"Are you sure we shouldn't call the police?" Brock asked from his corner of the sofa, drawing Cody's attention back to the current situation. His brother was cracking pistachio nuts over a bowl in the far corner of the living room, his eyes on the TV, which was muted and tuned to a baseball game.

Brock had a knack for appearing unconcerned. Unflappable. But Cody knew he did stuff like that—pour the nuts, watch the game—to distract himself from the tense energy that tended to spark at all their family gatherings.

"And say what? My wife didn't make dinner tonight?" Dad quit pacing and filled the coffeepot with water. "I saw her at breakfast this morning, and you know as well as I do they aren't going to do anything until she's been missing at least twenty-four hours."

Cody guessed the real reason he didn't call the

police was that he had a long-standing gripe with the local sheriff. But then, their father had never been an easy man to deal with. He had feuds with half of Laramie County.

"Here's Scarlett," Carson announced, getting to his feet as he looked out the window from behind Cody.

Cody watched a Mercedes limo pull up to the house. It had to be their grandfather's car. No one else rode around town in one of those. He hoped his dad wouldn't notice.

Maisie and Maddy emerged from the opposite end of the house. "I don't see anything out of place," Maisie told them. "Her suitcase is still here and there are no clothes or jewelry noticeably gone."

Impatient for their father to fill them in on what the hell was going on, Cody moved to the front door and opened it for Scarlett. Behind her, the limo drove away, its taillights disappearing up the access road.

"Nice ride," he muttered, but he tugged one of her curls as he said it. "Good to have you back."

A few minutes later they were all seated around the living room of what had been the foreman's quarters, a home Donovan had insisted on taking over once he gave the ranch duties to Cody. Brock ran his quarter horse breeding business primarily out of Creek Spill and had a home on the property. Maddy stayed at the White Canyon these days. Scarlett had a house at Black Creek and Maisie had built a tiny cabin for herself down at the creek's edge even though there was more than enough room for her at the main house.

They were a family, yes. But they'd all chosen their own niches, and carefully protected their space. It seemed to work well enough for everyone except Scarlett, who was chafing to move away. And maybe Carson, who was stuck in Cheyenne after his rodeo dreams had ended.

Their father cleared his throat. He was sitting on the edge of an old desk he'd been refurbishing in his spare time.

"I last saw Paige at breakfast this morning. You all know I've been concerned about her researching trips, when she's never expressed a desire to travel." He kept his phone clutched tightly in one hand, the only sign that he was upset. "Paige packed me a lunch, just like always, in case I had work in one of the far fields."

Cody thought about his stepmother's marriage to his father. She was much younger than Donovan, and he had never been an easy man to live with. Could she have decided to leave him?

She didn't have much family. Her parents had died in a car crash when she was a teen and she'd been on her own ever since. She'd been working in a bar in Cheyenne when she met Cody's father and started as a nanny to Cody, Carson and Brock after their mother's death.

"I called her at lunchtime and she didn't answer. She hasn't responded to my text messages all day. The car was gone when I got home for supper. I hoped maybe she forgot to pick up something for dinner and went to the store. But now I'm worried."

"Have you called any of her girlfriends?" Madeline asked. When her father shook his head, she volunteered to do that.

"What about family?" Scarlett asked.

They all stared at her.

"What?" She shrugged, picking at the flowers embroidered on the hem of her black skirt. "Just because she wasn't close with them doesn't mean she couldn't have decided to visit an aunt or an uncle. Do you know where any of her family lives, Dad?"

Cody thought it an odd question. Paige hadn't kept in touch with her extended family. No one had pressed her about it. It was something she had in common with Donovan. They didn't mind leaving the past behind and building a family of their own they could count on, consisting of the group assembled in the living room right now.

"Somewhere in northern Manitoba, I think. But she wouldn't turn to them." He shook his head, certain about that much.

"Have you tried tracking her phone?" Madeline asked. "Do you have any features like that on your plan?"

Their father stared at her blankly.

Cody stood from his seat by the front window, feeling restless. All the anxiety in the room only added to his own fears. "Dad, give Maddy your cell. She can tell if you have a program that shows where other devices on your phone plan are located."

Donovan passed the older model cell to Madeline, but Cody didn't hold out much hope. Neither his father nor stepmother liked their phones, using them mostly as photo albums.

"Are any of her things missing?" Brock asked, shifting to cross his ankles.

"No. Not that I can tell." Their father pursed his lips and looked around the room. The frown lines were etched deep in his tanned face. "Did she text any of you in the last twenty-four hours? Say anything unusual?"

Cody pulled out his phone to double-check, since Jillian had been the one to read through the slew of group messages this afternoon. But there was nothing from Paige.

There was silence for a moment until Scarlett spoke up. "She sent me a note last night telling me to be careful. But that's all."

Their father stared at his youngest daughter for a long moment. "She was worried about this trip. And she didn't like you seeing the actor."

"I didn't go to see Logan," Scarlett protested.

Cody barely grasped what they were talking about. And he only knew as much as he did thanks to Jillian. Funny that he had a better understanding of his family because of her, especially when she hardly knew them. She hadn't even met half of them. But then, maybe that was an indictment of him, and how he'd detached himself from the rest of the McNeills.

Maisie cleared her throat, slanting a glance at Scarlett.

"Okay, I went to see him, but only to tell him exactly what I think of self-important actors." Scarlett crossed her legs, the tulle of her flowered skirt swirling like a dark cloud around her knees.

Carson pinched the bridge of his nose. "Can we focus on Paige? Should we search the ranch?"

A surge of fear jolted Cody. The idea that she might be hurt somewhere on the property hadn't occurred to him. But their mother had died on the ranch.

"Good idea." Cody was already on his feet. "We should divide up the acreage and start looking."

Brock and Carson stood. Someone turned off the TV and Carson pulled up a map on his phone. Maisie was already claiming the terrain she would search on horseback, while Scarlett went to a closet to dig out flashlights. Cody noticed Maddy move to stand beside their father, an arm around his shoulders. The old man—who wasn't all that old—suddenly looked every one of his sixty years. If the thought of something happening to Paige made Cody's gut twist, he could only imagine what it did to his dad.

Once they'd all made a plan to check in with each other, Cody took his phone and his search assignment, then drove Scarlett to the stables, since she didn't have her car. Carson drove behind them. Cody planned to search on horseback, but he would insist that Scarlett take the Gator, so she could use the headlight. It would be safer for her.

"You okay?" he asked her on the way over to the stables near the main house. His gaze went to the bedroom window where Jillian's light was still on.

"I guess." Scarlett seemed nervous. Fidgety and hesitant. She must be really worried. "I just feel bad that Dad thinks Mom disappearing could have anything to do with me, or with my visit to LA. I knew she was worried but…" She shook her head. "Not any more worried than normal, right?"

"You're entitled to follow your dreams," he told her, realizing he meant it even though he'd gotten the idea from Jillian. "Dad and Paige both know that, even if they guilt-trip you about it."

Cody was trying to reassure her, but she still seemed upset. After he parked the truck between the equipment building and the stables, he gave her a hug with one arm.

"She's going to be fine," he told her. "We'll find Paige."

A little while later, as he saddled up his horse to start his search, he hoped that was true. He had thought the most likely scenario was that Paige had left Dad. Maybe they'd had an argument or something that Dad wouldn't own up to. But mounting a search of the property in the dark brought home the reality that something could have happened to her.

The fear in his gut wasn't just about Paige. This night only heightened his sense that Jillian and his child seemed so vulnerable, too. Tomorrow, he would ask Jillian what she needed to be happy in Cheyenne. How he could help her find fulfillment—to pursue her dreams—from Wyoming.

There was nothing more important to him in the world than keeping her and his baby safe.

Twelve

Jillian was awake when Cody returned to the main house at midnight. He'd messaged her earlier to let her know about Paige's disappearance and the search. So when Jillian saw the pickup truck's headlights in the driveway from her window, she rushed downstairs to see if they'd found his stepmother.

She reached the kitchen as he was coming through the front door. His expression was even more somber than usual, and her chest tightened.

"Any word?" she asked, flipping on the light over the oven range to illuminate the kitchen.

"Jillian." His broad shoulders sagged a bit as he saw her. "I didn't want to wake you."

She noticed now that he'd slid off his boots at the door. He padded over to her in his socks, barely making a sound on the hardwood floor.

"I've been worried." She reached to touch him, to offer what comfort she could.

He wrapped her in his arms and kissed her. Fast. Hard. She could feel the tension in him, and the worry. She pressed herself closer, breathing him in. For a span of two heartbeats, she kissed him back, wanting him. Wishing she could lose herself in his touch.

But then, she edged back, knowing they needed to talk.

His gaze held hers for a long moment, his breathing harsh. Then he straightened.

"We halted the search when Paige called Madeline shortly before midnight. She'd decided to drive to Yellowstone to clear her head in the mountains for a few days." Cody edged back to look down at Jillian, his hands rubbing warmth into her upper arms, making her realize she'd forgotten her robe in her rush to get downstairs.

Fresh awareness sparked inside her at his touch.

"Why didn't she answer her cell all day?" Some of the worry slid away at the news that his stepmother was safe, but Jillian wondered why he still seemed so on edge.

She could feel the tension in his shoulders where her hands lingered, and she wanted to ease that away. To curl against him all night long. How was it possible that someone she'd known for such a short amount of time could feel so right beside her?

"She said she forgot it at a rest stop off the highway on the way there. She called from a hotel phone." Frowning, he slid his hand to Jillian's back, gently steering her out of the kitchen. "I'll tell you more once you're in bed. You need your rest."

"Why did she call Madeline and not your father?" she asked, leading him up the stairs toward the room where she'd been sleeping the past two nights.

"I don't know. They didn't talk long, I guess because she was tired. But she told Maddy she'd attended a yoga retreat up there once, and she thought the meditation would be good for her after a stressful week."

"Because of the film shoot?" Jillian couldn't help feeling a twinge of guilt over that. Had the promise of outsiders descending on Paige's home been that upsetting? "I only went ahead with booking the site when your siblings were all on board. It didn't occur to me—"

"It's not your fault. I'm guessing she had a falling out with my father or she would have phoned him." Cody pushed open her bedroom door, accompanying her inside.

The ritual of it, of being in his house, of waiting for him to come home, felt intimate. As did sliding between her sheets when he lifted the blanket for her. Pleasurable shivers chased one another up and down her spine. The heated look in his blue eyes as he pulled the covers up to her chin told her that he was feeling some of those same things.

Attraction, yes. But more than that, connection.

It hadn't been there for him the last time they'd

shared a bed, but a hopeful piece of her heart clamored to know—if she lay with him again, would the bond be there this time?

She knew this wasn't the right time to think about those things. He was exhausted from worry. And they'd both had plenty to think about before the news about Paige.

"What did your father have to say?" she asked.

"I didn't see him after Maddy called to update me. I came straight here from the search." Cody shook his head, the weariness evident in his voice as he sat on the edge of the mattress.

"We can talk more in the morning." She lifted her hand to his cheek on impulse, her feelings for this man in a hopeless tangle.

The father of her child.

"Of course." His nod was so automatic, so agreeable, she wondered again if the tenderness was for the baby's sake.

A twinge of hurt forced her hand away, and she reminded herself she would be leaving soon. She'd already committed to her next job, to help ensure she didn't weaken where Cody was concerned. She knew how vulnerable her heart would be to this man if she wasn't careful.

"I need to go to Creek Spill tomorrow afternoon to review a few final details with Carson." She swallowed hard, telling herself it would get easier one day to have a relationship with Cody. A platonic relationship. A functional, co-parenting agreement.

"I'll drive you over there," he offered, his fingers sifting absently through her hair, stirring a hunger for him she couldn't imagine would ever be sated.

The passion that had been there since that first night remained, stronger than ever. But was it fair to lose herself in all that heat when she lost a piece of her heart to him every time?

That was exactly why being around him was so dangerous to her.

"There's no need. I'm just introducing him to the assistant director. And I have a few more questions about storing equipment for the shoot."

Cody lingered another moment, his fingers

tracing the line of her jaw as he stared down into her eyes. Her breath caught. Held.

"I want to spend as much time as I can with you while we figure out what's next for us, Jillian. Let me drive you."

She could hardly refuse. If anything, she respected him all the more for his determination to get to know her better. To pave the way for their child's future.

At her nod, he brushed his fingers over her curls one last time, then bade her good-night. Sensation tingled through her scalp long after he left, his touch filtering into her dreams and arousing desire she needed desperately to forget.

Cody couldn't take his eyes off Jillian the next day as she walked around Carson's ranch with the assistant director, Leon Wells. Her laughter floated on the breeze, her joy in simple things infectious as she pointed out patches of ordinary wildflowers or mountain views. It was hard to believe that the movie crew would be shooting at the Creek Spill Ranch as early as next week.

Weather permitting.

It seemed that the assistant director followed the weather like a meteorologist. When they'd all convened at the Creek Spill ranch house earlier this afternoon, the man had asked a dozen questions about Wyoming's climate, and had proceeded to speculate on cloud formation and humidity levels for ten days out, apparently needing as much information as possible to get the shots he wanted.

The discussion around Carson's kitchen table had been more interesting than Cody had anticipated. It also made him realize how long it had been since he'd set foot in his brother's house. The rift between them had grown worse with their grandfather's arrival, but as the weeks dragged on and Malcolm McNeill maintained a presence in Cheyenne, Cody realized he couldn't afford to alienate more members of his family. Especially with a child on the way. He needed to think about building relationships.

Now, while Jillian walked around the yard and outbuildings with Leon Wells, Cody forced his attention away from her and turned to his twin. Carson was bent over the engine of an old pickup truck that had seen better days.

He liked to fix things. Cody had forgotten that about his brother in the years they'd lived apart. From broken televisions to failed sump pumps, Carson was drawn to all things mechanical. He'd never thrown away something that could be fixed with a replacement part bought online, a talent that made him popular among the ranch hands. Cody would bet the truck belonged to one of the local cowboys who couldn't afford to replace it.

"You think Dad and Paige had a falling out?" Cody asked, keeping one eye on Jillian while he bent over the engine by his brother.

"Hard to say. One's about as chatty as the other."

"You're right about that," Cody mused, using a nearby rag to clean up connections on the battery terminal that were caked with rust. "Something's got Paige freaked out."

"The girls know more than they're saying." Carson passed him a bottle of lemon juice, barely looking up from where he was wrestling with a new timing belt.

"You think?" Cody hadn't gotten that impression. They'd all seemed worried last night. He used the lemon juice on the terminals.

"Just a hunch. Maisie and Scarlett were deep in conversation when I stopped by Maisie's place this morning. But they went quiet when I arrived." Carson tugged the new belt into place and straightened, stretching his forearms from the effort. "Are you going to be okay with this film shoot?"

The question surprised him. "A bit late in the game for me to give my blessing."

"It's happening either way. But I guess I hoped spending time with Jillian was making you more amenable to the idea." Carson's gaze went to her and the assistant director, who were coming toward them.

As Cody watched Jillian, her red hair tipped with gold in the sunlight, he realized how little the film mattered in the big scheme of things. This woman was important to him. The movie, the family drama, even the rift with his grand-father—none of it mattered half as much as Jillian Ross and their child.

All he wanted was for her to stay safe, healthy and with him. Already he could imagine a future of more rodeos. More dances in dive bars. More nights spent with her in his arms.

"She's important to me," he confided to his brother. "So if it makes her happy, I'll have to get on board."

Carson's easy smile was a sight Cody hadn't seen in a while.

"They have a way of changing our priorities in a hurry, don't they?" He clapped Cody on the back just as Jillian and Leon rejoined them.

"All set?" Cody asked her, ready to take her home. To have her all to himself.

"I am." Her eyes lingered on his, and he realized the heat that had started to burn that first night had only grown hotter.

He wanted to prepare a picnic for supper and drive her out to his favorite spot to view the stars while the weather was mild.

The assistant director, a skinny young man with wire-rimmed glasses, stepped forward, his dress shirt drenched in sweat and clinging to his shoulders in the summer heat.

"It's been nice meeting you." Leon shook Cody's hand and then Carson's, before turning back to Jillian. "And Alyssa told me you've got a fun assignment coming up next. Safe travels to Flagstaff, Jillian."

Cody wondered if he'd just misheard the man.

Of course. He *must* have misheard. Or maybe misunderstood. Because Jillian couldn't be going anywhere.

"Flagstaff?" Cody turned to face Jillian. Leon was already hurrying toward his white rental car. Carson had stalked off, too, his whistle fading as he headed toward the horse barn.

Jillian's face was pale. Her lips pursed. "I was going to talk to you about that."

His stomach fell like a stone.

"About Arizona?" he asked, his brain working overtime to fit pieces together that made no sense. "You're pregnant."

"I know that. But I still have a job to do, Cody. And putting my feet up for nine more months isn't going to ensure a healthy child. If anything, I should stay active and exercise."

He was vaguely aware of Leon's car as the assistant director drove away from Creek Spill. Birds circled overhead, casting shadows on the grass.

"You have a higher risk for recurrence." He'd read and reread his copies of the literature from all the doctors they'd seen. "You need to be careful. We can stack the odds in your favor with a more relaxed lifestyle. Less stress."

Maybe he wasn't fighting fair to remind her of those things. But damn it. She couldn't leave. Not now.

"The baby is not at risk," she reminded him, her voice steely.

As if that was all that mattered to him.

"But you are," he repeated, his heart pounding. Fear chilled the sweat on his skin. How could she even consider walking away? "Jillian, why not do everything in our power to ensure you stay healthy?"

They weren't the romantic words he wanted to give her. But she'd forced his hand. Hadn't given him enough time to woo her. To win her forever.

"I will." She laid a hand on his chest, her touch stirring desire despite the way things were falling apart all around them. "I promise you, I will. But I can't stop living just because there's a chance cancer will come back. I won't spend my life cowering in fear of what-ifs that are out of my control."

Something in those beautiful hazel eyes told him that her mind was made up. He felt like the ground had just given way beneath him.

"How long have you known you're leaving?" He couldn't catch his breath, the sense of betrayal rising right alongside the fear.

They'd only just started to really know each other. To build something on top of all that heat and passion.

"I've been prepared to spend the whole week

here so we can come up with a plan for co-parenting—"

"Is that what this week was going to be about for you?" He thought about all the plans he'd made. The picnic under the stars. A drive up to Yellowstone to show her the sights, followed by a candlelight dinner.

None of his ideas had involved a co-parenting plan. They were all about *her*. Even now, he wanted to haul her into his arms and kiss her. Remind her how good they were together.

"How long have you known you're leaving?" He repeated the question because he needed an answer.

He had to know how long she'd been plotting her getaway while he charted out a future together. A future she didn't want any part of.

"I just committed to the assignment last night." Her palm fell away from his chest.

He missed her touch already. But damn it, her hand wasn't the only thing slipping away.

"Jillian, don't do this. Don't shut me out." He reached for anything to make her stay, caught on his worst fear. "What if something happens to you? How will I raise this child by myself?" He couldn't afford to lose her. The idea cracked open an ache inside him, one that no amount of words could soothe.

"I hope you won't have to." Her eyes glittered in the sunlight, and he knew she was hurting, too. "But if it came to that, I know you could."

So that was it?

They stared at each other under the cloudless blue sky. Cody couldn't imagine a worse pain than that. He had lost his own mother as a child. He knew exactly how big a scar it left. Anger stirred.

"I can't believe you would choose some superficial adventures over this—the chance to be a family." He'd thought family was more important to her than that. She'd said she envied his.

She huffed out an exasperated sigh.

"It's not about that. We hardly know each other. We can't force ourselves to be a family when we're not ready. I won't be another responsibility weighing you down."

The gulf between them widened. And Cody didn't have a single idea how to bridge it.

While hope dried up to nothing, he became aware of his brother running toward them.

Running?

Jillian turned toward Carson, too. He was just fifteen yards away, waving a hand over his head, flagging their attention.

"We need to get to the hospital," he called to them, his cell phone in one hand while he pulled his keys from his jeans pocket. "Paige has been in an accident."

Thirteen

Scarlett couldn't catch her breath.

A panic attack was coming and she couldn't stop it as she paced around the women's bathroom at Eastern Idaho Regional Medical Center, clutching her phone and waiting for word on her mother's condition following emergency surgery. According to the report from the emergency techs who brought her in, a sudden rainstorm had created dangerous conditions on a trail where Paige had been hiking that morning, and she'd slipped down a mountainside. She had to be rescued by horseback and then airlifted to the nearest trauma center with a fractured hip and tibia.

The last few hours had been a blur, but at least they'd all made it to the hospital as fast as possible. It would have been nine hours away by car, but because Malcolm McNeill had sent his plane back to the private airfield outside Cheyenne, Scarlett and her family were able to fly. They'd been in the air for only an hour, but it had seemed endless. Brock had stayed behind to tend to some business at the White Canyon Ranch for Madeline so she could be with Paige. But all the other siblings had come.

Maisie plowed through the swinging bathroom door.

"I got your text…" She rushed over as soon as she got a look at Scarlett. "Are you okay?"

Scarlett shook her head. "I think—" she breathed faster "—I'm hyperventilating."

Maisie squeezed her. "You're okay." She spoke slowly. "I want you to hold your breath, honey. Just clamp down and hold it."

Scarlett sucked in air and tried not to breathe

out, watching her sister. Keeping her eyes on Maisie, who always knew what to do. Those deep blue eyes grounded her. Helped her.

When the air rushed out again, Maisie nodded. "That's okay. This time purse your lips. Like this." She scrunched her lips tight. "That way you can slow the exhale, okay?"

Scarlett followed instructions. She could feel her heart rate slowing. She was calming down. Oxygen was flowing to her brain again. She nodded.

"I'm okay," she said finally. "Thanks for coming in. I just got in a panic thinking about that note. How am I ever going to tell everyone about it?"

She'd shown it to Maisie last night during the search for their mother. Scarlett had been ready to show it to her whole family. But once they'd learned Paige was safe, Maisie had told her it would be okay to sit on the note until they could show it to their mom. Give her a chance to respond before getting their father involved, just in case the message was something that could hurt their marriage.

"You haven't done anything wrong." Maisie combed her fingers through Scarlett's hair before tugging her toward the mirror. "Come here." She wet a paper towel.

"Dad and Cody will say I should have told them last night." Scarlett peered into the mirror at her smeared mascara. Her eyes were bloodshot from lack of sleep.

"Coulda, shoulda, woulda," Maisie chanted as she dabbed away the mascara streaks, meeting Scarlett's eyes in the mirror. "Doesn't matter now. Just go out there and share it. Let them weigh in. This is not your burden alone, okay? They deserve to know so they can help figure out what to do."

"Right." Scarlett nodded. "How would anyone who doesn't know our family know that I was in LA? I just keep wondering how that guy knew where to find me."

"Your friend Lucie knew you were going. She could have told someone." Maisie rubbed her cheek hard to get a spot off. "Logan could have heard you'd be there. And he's the one who actually handed it to you."

Scarlett's heart sank. "No."

"He's involved with the film, too," Maisie insisted, making perfect, logical sense. "And don't forget the note isn't just about Mom. Someone clearly doesn't want *Winning the West* to be filmed in Cheyenne."

But it couldn't be Logan. That theory would make more sense if he was trying to avoid Scarlett. But based on what he'd said when he'd followed her out of the club, he hadn't meant to break things off with her in the first place. She couldn't deny a tiny piece of her wished those words were true. For her family's sake, though, she wouldn't take chances.

"All the more reason to be on my guard when the film starts shooting." Taking the paper towel from her sister, Scarlett finished cleaning up her face. "I'm ready. I need to go tell them."

Jillian's head throbbed with worry as she sat next to Cody in the busy trauma center's waiting room. Donovan McNeill paced near a window, pausing now and again to drum his fist gently on the glass or to slouch in a seat nearby. Cody and Carson sat on opposite sides of the room, their tense shoulders and jutting jaws like matching bookends of worry.

The hospital had to bring up tough feelings for them both. They'd lost their own mother to her injuries from the bull.

Jillian had never questioned whether she would make the trip with him or not. Although now, looking back at the last few frightening hours, she wondered if that had been the right decision. Maybe she didn't belong here.

Yet even while things were falling apart between her and Cody, she couldn't turn her back on the McNeills. Not when she carried Cody's heir. Not after seeing the way they pulled together, even when it hurt. When Paige had been missing, Cody and Carson had even set aside their differences to search for her.

Donovan McNeill hadn't thought twice about accepting his father's plane when it meant getting to his wife's bedside, and from what Jillian could gather, he hadn't spoken to Malcolm in over twenty-five years. It was moments like this that brought people together and made crystal clear what was really important in life.

And for Jillian, she couldn't imagine being anywhere else right now. Everything she'd spouted to Cody about pursuing dreams paled in comparison to being beside him when he needed her. She wanted to be right here. With him. With her child's family.

The institutional clock on the wall ticked audibly, even over the hum of activity all around them. The nurses' station monitors beeped at regular intervals. The steady sound of machinery helping struggling human bodies to function was strangely reassuring.

Maisie and Scarlett were just returning from the bathroom. Had Scarlett been crying? Her face looked puffy and red.

"Family of Paige McNeill?" a gray-haired doctor in green scrubs called out as he exited one of the doors marked Do Not Enter.

As one, seven people tensed.

The siblings seemed to realize it was their father's right to speak to the doctor, so they waited while Donovan strode over to him first. But Jillian and Cody were close enough to overhear the conversation. And the others crowded closer, behind their father.

"The surgery went well," the doctor assured him. "I was worried about the hip, but I'm pleased with how well the fracture set. The tibia gave us no trouble. We might find more damage in her left arm that needs attention, but we've splinted it and want her to heal from the trauma of the fall before we work on anything else."

A sigh of relief echoed around the group.

"Can we see her?" Donovan asked, raking a hand through his salt-and-pepper hair.

"She won't come out of the anesthesia for a while, but you're welcome to sit with her in the recovery room. Only one at a time, though, I'm afraid." His gray eyebrows swooped down. "Her condition is still critical."

Donovan nodded. Cody rose and interjected,

"Doctor, what about her head? Did she hit it in the fall?"

The surgeon nodded in turn, as if the question was expected. "There is very little external damage and her scans look clear, but she definitely hit her temple, so we'll be monitoring her closely for problems. She's on a ventilator and she's been sedated because of the trauma. She might not be able to communicate much even after the anesthesia wears off." Excusing himself, the doctor left, pointing them toward a small vestibule outside the recovery area.

Donovan turned to Madeline, clapping a hand on her shoulder. "We can trade off sitting with her once she wakes up, but I'd like to go in there first."

No one argued with him as the rest of the family relocated to the quieter waiting area.

"It's good news, though, right?" Madeline asked.

When no one else said anything, Jillian gave her shoulders a hug. "I think so."

Jillian had barely settled in her seat next to Cody when Maisie leaned forward in her chair.

"I know we're all worried about Mom. But now that Dad's gone, Scarlett has something to share." She leveled a stare at her sister.

Cody straightened in his seat. Jillian found herself reaching for him. Her fingers threading through his on instinct.

Scarlett's cheeks went pink. "With all that was going on, I didn't know when to bring this up." She reached into her purse and withdrew a folded piece of paper. Her hands were unsteady as she smoothed the wrinkles and flattened it with her hand before continuing.

"When I was in Hollywood, some guy I never met before tried to hand me this note." She kept her voice quiet even though there was no one else around in the waiting area.

She passed the note to Cody first.

As she read it over his shoulder, Jillian's gut clenched. For Cody. For Paige. For all of them. And what did her film have to do with any of it?

Cody swore softly as he read and quickly

passed the note to Carson. Madeline moved closer to read it with him. Maisie had obviously already seen it.

"Why the hell didn't you tell us about this last night when Paige went missing?" Cody demanded. Anger had crept into his voice, though he didn't raise it.

Jillian wondered the same thing.

"Scarlett told me," Maisie retorted, her posture defensive as she moved to shield her sister. "And we were about to bring it to Dad when Mom called home. We had hoped to ask her about it first."

Cody took a deep breath and changed his approach. "I get it. You were worried your mother had good reason for hiding something about her past from Dad. But what if the person who gave you this note intends to hurt her? What if someone already did?"

Scarlett leaned forward in her chair. "It doesn't read like a physical threat. And blackmail isn't usually that kind of crime."

"Do you think this is blackmail?" Jillian asked, trying to make sense of it.

At the same time, Carson said, "Would you recognize the guy who gave this to you if you saw him again?"

"I wouldn't recognize him." Scarlett shook her head, her long dark curls drooping. All the Mc-Neills looked the worse for wear after the hours of uncertainty, but Scarlett seemed even more bedraggled. Maybe she hadn't slept well with the weight of the letter on her mind.

"Your friend might," Maisie said, turning to the rest of the family. "Scarlett was with Logan when it happened. He saw the guy, too."

"Should we tell Dad?" Scarlett asked. "I just don't want to pile too much on him now."

Cody was the first to answer. "We tell him as soon as she wakes up."

Beside him, Carson nodded, cementing the decision.

"If someone is trying to make trouble for us, we all need to be on guard," Carson added. "I wouldn't have agreed to the film if I'd known."

Scarlett looked miserable. "I didn't get this until afterward."

Maisie jumped to her little sister's defense again, and while she explained to Carson all the reasons this was a difficult position for Scarlett, Cody leaned over to speak in Jillian's ear.

"Walk with me?"

It was a question, but he was already pulling her to her feet. Grateful for the suggestion, Jillian followed him.

"We'll be back in ten," Cody announced over his shoulder. He placed a hand on the small of her back, guiding her out the door of the private waiting room and back into the frenzy of the trauma floor.

But a few moments later, they were walking down a long corridor toward a door with a small green sign pointing the way to the meditation garden. It was sponsored by a local nursery.

"I needed some air." His voice rasped with exhaustion even though it was only eight o'clock.

Neither of them had slept much the night before.

"Me, too." She stepped out into a sweet-smelling garden half covered with a white pergola. Jasmine hung over the arches, the fragrance heavy in the fresh air.

Cody guided them toward a bench near a bubbling fountain with a statue of a little girl reaching into a stream of running water. The sun had just set, but landscape lights and the moon made it easy to see.

"How are you feeling?" He led her to the bench and they sat down side by side.

The sound of water rushing from the fountain into a small pond soothed her.

Or maybe it was the presence of the man beside her. A man who meant more to her with each passing hour. Their lives had become intertwined so fast, fueled by the adrenaline of their life circumstances—her illness, his family. And somehow, they'd found something special.

Something she wasn't ready to turn her back on.

"Physically, I'm fine." She turned and glanced up at him. "Emotionally drained, as I'm sure you are, too." She put her hand on his knee. "I hope it wasn't presumptuous of me to make the trip here with your family."

"I'm glad you're here, Jillian." He slid his fingers around hers, his touch warming her as it had from that first night when they'd danced. "If it was up to me, you'd be staying in Cheyenne." He looked up at the stars for a long moment before his eyes locked on hers. "Spending time with me and my family. Giving us a chance to grow on you."

Her throat burned at the picture he painted. As if it was that simple. She picked at a tendril of jasmine that curled around the arm of the bench, traced the veins in one green leaf.

"Cody, I know how fast you'd all grow on me if I stay in Cheyenne." But she'd given her love to someone before, only to discover at the cruelest possible moment how much it could hurt to find that love was one-sided.

Cody was too honorable a man to pretend a devotion he didn't feel. But Jillian would never know if his tender concern was all for the sake of his child. His heir.

The tiny life that had only just begun to grow.

"Then why won't you?" The hurt and confusion in his voice forced her to be honest.

To share her hurts, too.

She let go of the jasmine and looked him in the eye. "Because I can't bear to fall in love with you and know you only wanted me here for the sake of this baby."

His eyes closed as if she'd dealt him a blow. When he opened them, they were clearer. Determined.

"You faced cancer alone. You scrapped the whole direction of your life to start over again. You got a dream job by sheer force of will. And you waltzed into Cheyenne and took on the most formidable McNeill in town to get what you wanted." He lifted her hands in both of his as he stared into her eyes. "Don't you dare tell me you're too scared to fall in love with me."

A shocked laugh escaped her. Or maybe it was a little bit of hysteria edging through after the upheaval of the last few days.

"A woman has her limits." She felt tears bubbling up, but didn't want to shed them. "There's so much out of my control—"

"But you can control this? Us?" He brought her hand to his face and laid it along his jaw, kissing the palm. "That's the worst thing to try to dictate. You can't tell your heart what to feel."

The breeze stirred a flag over their heads, the fabric snapping in the wind. She struggled to keep her wits about her. To look at this relationship rationally and not through the eyes of a woman in love. She couldn't afford that kind of weakness now.

"I can try to protect it," she argued weakly, feeling her defenses slide away and helpless to resurrect them.

He shook his head, sadness and regret in his eyes. "Can I tell you a secret? It's going to sound awful to say, but my father has been protecting his heart ever since my mother died."

Jillian blinked in surprise. An older couple strolled past them, arm in arm, and disappeared into the grounds beyond the garden.

"What about Paige?" She couldn't imagine putting her heart in Cody's hands if she wasn't certain he would give her his in return. But maybe some women could love that way.

"A marriage of convenience. I always knew why my father chose her—she took care of his kids, no questions asked. But until I read that note Scarlett showed us, it never occurred to me Paige might have been running from demons of her own when she agreed to marry Dad."

Jillian shivered. "I couldn't bear a lifetime of loneliness like that."

"There's still time for them." Cody glanced toward the hospital. "I sure as hell hope so, anyway." He turned to her again. "But my point is this. Protecting your heart is what leads to the real hurt. To the emptiness of never really connecting with people."

"So your advice to me is that I should open my heart to you."

"Obviously." He grinned, and for a moment it was that same easy grin as his brother's, the smile that had captivated her that first night at the bar. Except it was all his. Uniquely Cody. "But what

I'm really trying to say is that I would never trap either one of us in that kind of relationship. If it doesn't work, we'll find a way to love our child as equals and friends."

Her heart hurt at the idea of walking away. Of trying at love and failing.

On the far side of the hospital, an ambulance siren blared, a surge of urgency sounding through the otherwise peaceful retreat.

"I want more than that for this baby." Her hand crept to her flat belly, where she prayed their child would grow.

"So do I." He tipped his forehead to hers. "Family means everything to me, Jillian."

"I don't want you to force yourself to love me."

"You wouldn't be forcing me." He shook his head, certainty in his eyes. "My feelings for you are so real, I can't imagine a life without you. And I don't know how that happened so fast, but it did."

She blinked, struggling to follow what he was saying. "Do you mean—"

"Wait." He pressed a finger to her lips. Gently.

"Let me get this out while I can. I don't want to rush you, Jillian. But I love you, and I don't want you to leave."

Her heart melted. Or maybe it was all her doubts that slid away at his words—words he would never utter unless he meant them. Happiness unfurled like a spring bloom, but before she could answer, he rushed on, continuing, "And we can date first, you know, if you aren't ready for more. Take it one day at a time. But we can only do that if we're in the same state."

"You don't want me to go to Flagstaff." She understood what he was asking. Recognized the practical limitations of being a rancher. He was tied to the land.

"I didn't say that. If you go, I go with you." He kissed her cheek.

Then the other.

Her pulse rate doubled as she thought through his words, felt the rasp of his unshaved face against her skin.

"You would do that for me?" That alone told

her so much about his commitment to her. To this love.

"Without a moment's hesitation." He wasn't a man to tease. And he sure wouldn't lie about something like that.

But she had to think of his wants, as well. "I love you, Cody. And I love that you would do that for me. But you're a rancher. How could you leave the ranch?"

She appreciated that earthiness about him. The way he embraced the land and wasn't pretentious in spite of his vast fortune. She didn't want to change him.

"I like to think of myself as a rancher, Jillian. But first and foremost, I am a McNeill." He said it like that explained everything. But even though she'd researched his lands for the film, she'd never read much about his family's assets or wealth.

"I know your grandfather is rich," she began, thinking through what he was saying. "He's the head of McNeill Resorts."

"Yes. And my father has spent his whole life

trying to outshine his old man because of an old feud that stopped mattering a long time ago. While I prefer to live off what I earn on the ranch, I have enough other holdings that I could take some time away from Cheyenne while we see the world. Check off some of those adventures on your list." He leaned in to kiss her lips with infinite tenderness. "Together."

She couldn't have been more stunned.

Biting her lip, she tasted his kiss on her mouth. She hardly dared to believe what he was offering her.

"That would be amazing." She felt light. Free. Loved.

Her heart soared high and she didn't try to stop it. She simply let the joy fill her up.

"You have to let me take care of you, though. Good food. Enough rest." He kissed her again, lingering this time until her body heated with awareness. "And if I opt to spend the day in bed with you, you have to tell me if I wear you out."

She leaned back long enough to see the wicked gleam in his eyes. She nipped his ear in retaliation before she whispered, "I bet I'll wear you out first."

"Are we really going to do this, Jillian? Conquer the world and that list of adventures together?" His eyes were serious again. "Hearing about Paige today, knowing how fragile life can be—" He swallowed hard and kissed her again. "I don't want to waste a day being away from you."

With all her heart, Jillian hoped she could fulfill this man's dreams. But if nothing else, she was going to try to make him happy for as much time as they had together. And yes, she was going to let herself fall head over heels for him.

She guessed the woozy feeling she had meant it was already happening.

"I won't waste a minute," she promised.

And kissed him with abandon, treasuring the promise of tomorrow with the worthiest man she'd ever met.

* * * * *

LET'S TALK

Romance

For exclusive extracts, competitions and special offers, find us online:

f facebook.com/millsandboon

⊙ @millsandboonuk

🐦 @millsandboon

Or get in touch on 0844 844 1351*

For all the latest titles coming soon, visit millsandboon.co.uk/nextmonth